Henry Nehemiah Dodge

Three Crowns

Henry Nehemiah Dodge

Three Crowns

ISBN/EAN: 9783337266882

Printed in Europe, USA, Canada, Australia, Japan

Cover: Foto ©Andreas Hilbeck / pixelio.de

More available books at **www.hansebooks.com**

THREE CROWNS.

By the Author of

"CHRISTUS VICTOR."

BOSTON:

WILLIAM V. SPENCER.

1866.

CONTENTS.

	PAGE.
MARGRET	1
PAUL AND BERNARD	38
KASPAR AND GERTRUDE	92

THREE CROWNS.

MARGRET.

It is not dark, although the sun has set:
A faint and rosy light is lingering yet,
In air, on earth, and sea, o'er hill and plain, —
The promise of the sun to come again.

'Tis summer: at an open window stands
A lady with a letter in her hands;
There is no sorrow yet upon her face, —
As yet no bitter tears have left their trace.

She looks like one who has not waked to life;
Who stands as yet outside its rush and strife:
She is not dead nor cold; she slumbers now, —
Repose in life is written on her brow.

You see the fuel for the fire is there;
It needeth but the match to flame and flare:
The pulses of that heart can bound and leap;
Now beating gently as a child's in sleep.

And yet the letter that she's holding there,
Is big with fate for her and one elsewhere :
" This answer pleases him, so I'm content."
She murmurs, " What I've written must be sent."

She finds her messenger, who speeds away ;
And then returns to watch departing day :
She looks towards the sea, and murmurs low,
It makes me happy to relieve his woe.

How sweet it is to soothe another's pain,
To wake the sunlight in a heart again !
He wrote, I have not smiled since that sad day
I said, She loves me not, and sailed away.

Poor Philip, tossing on that restless sea,
This letter will bring peace and joy to thee !
I think that with my lot I am content,
Great happiness for me perhaps not meant.

I think in time I shall love Philip well :
I think our souls in harmony can dwell ;
That mighty Passion which has swayed the world,
And souls of men from life to death has hurled,

In mercy, I must think, has passed me by ;
I have not felt its grasp of agony :
My love is quiet, feeleth no alarm,
Knoweth no ecstasy, feareth no harm.

With Philip, I am master of my life :
Though I will be a loved, obedient wife,
I sometimes wonder if another soul
Could wrest the helm from me, and take control,

And at his pleasure make me sink or swim,
Hoist sail or anchor at a word from him :
Oh what a fearful power for man to hold,
Unless his soul by God's high hand controlled !

My Philip says, with me alone the power
To shield and save him in temptation's hour ;
He says that I am far more strong than he :
'Tis sometimes thus ; but ought it so to be ?

Did I say ought, since God alone doth give
The strength by which we help the weak to live ?
If He makes strong, shall I prefer to be
A woman weak because it pleaseth me ?

I shall have God to lean upon, and guide :
If Philip falters, Christ is at my side ;
My husband's faults shall be forgot in love ;
All human strength is weakness seen above.

We know Christ lighteth every soul that comes
Into this world : sometimes that light becomes
Feeble and dim ; Christ lays his royal hand
Upon some child of earth, with this command : —

Go thou, and tend for me that sacred fire ;
Watch well, and see the flame doth not expire :
Thy hand is feeble, but I'll hold it firm :
How strong thou art through me, I'll make thee learn.

Perhaps Christ gives a charge like that to me ;
I hold such thought in deep humility :
I feel. I think I have decided right :
At least for him I've made great darkness light.

    Sleep soft and well, my sailor brave,
      Upon the moonlit sea ;
    Into a faithful hand I gave
      A word from me to thee.

    Dream of a hope at last fulfilled,
      Of love that will abide ;
    Dream of a storm that has been stilled,
      Dream of a turning tide.

    Dream thy great wave of love and tears
      Has broken on the shore,
    But at the feet of one who hears
      And bids thee weep no more.

    Dream of a heart that will not shrink
      From any form of ill ;
    Though in a gulf of woe should sink,
      Be faithful to thee still.

How beautiful the Earth doth look to-night!
He seems enamoured with the moon's pale light;
Drinking it in at every hungry pore,
As if they two had never met before.

He seems so ready to forget, forgive
How oft the treacherous lady makes him grieve;
Why treacherous? Earth's heart is very wide;
She cannot always shine on every side.

If she is frowning here, she's smiling there:
I think we do belie the lady fair;
Perhaps behind a cloud she hides her face,
That she may witness not the Earth's disgrace.

She turns in loathing from some dreadful crime,
And sails away to light another clime;
They say it is the same where'er she goes,
Earth groans and bleeds and bends beneath his woes.

Can it be true there's so much grief on earth?
With me at least it has not come to birth.
I lift my heart in gratitude to Heaven;
To me on earth at least a life is given.

Quite easy now it seems to turn aside
From the broad pathway dangerous and wide:
I do not think that any human love
Could make me turn my face from God above.

Could love be turned to hatred in my heart?
A sweet affection prove a poisoned dart?
If I should have no right my head to lay
Upon a breast beloved, could I not pray

She might be spared and blest who slumbered there?
Should I not have the strength that sight to bear?
They say such things have driven women mad:
I cannot tell; these thoughts have made me sad.

I am oppressed with grief:
Father. give me relief.
Speak to my soul;
Tell me Thou wilt prevail:
If sin should me assail,
The storm control.

These fears are new to me.
But I am known to Thee:
Draw near, draw near:
I thought I loved Thee well;
Alas! I cannot tell
If Thou art here.

Here in this heart of mine.
I thought was wholly Thine.
What proof have I,
If sin should come to me,
I should victorious be,
That I should fly

To Thee, and be content
With that thy love had sent,
　　Though hard to bear ;
If slain, should love Thee still,
And to Thy holy will
　　Bow down in prayer?

Oh, let no human face
Take that accursed place
　　'Tween Thee and me !
Let not man stand between,
A fatal, damning screen,
　　The soul and Thee.

However grand he be,
Thou must be first with me ;
　　He must go down :
Be he of royal birth,
'Tis not for child of earth
　　To wear that crown.

If passion is so strong,
Doth not to Thee belong
　　Still greater strength?
Must not Earth's deadliest foes
Yield, after sternest blows,
　　To Thee at length?

Ah, no ! I will not fear :
Thou hast not placed us here
　　To faint and fall ;

> This mighty, human love
> Speaks of the God above,
>   Stronger than all.

She rises from her knees; peace has returned, —
That childlike faith in good for which she yearned:
"Whence came this storm of fear which shook me so.
I who have never felt the touch of woe?

I will not think such tragedies are done
Upon this brave old world beneath the sun;
I'll not believe men sin and suffer so:
These human lives through blood and fire flow.

Now I will think of Philip; trust that we
May sail in peace across a summer sea.
Must the waves roar and fatal storms arise
To make the sailor lift to Heaven his eyes?

Must there be tempest, shipwreck, mortal fear,
To make him glad to know the harbor near?
I cannot tell: I know I'm not afraid
To trust to God the hearts that He has made."

———————

Two months sped on; no outward change had come
Upon the quiet life of Margret's home:
Philip had written that he could not tell
How blessed he was, how happy, and how well.

The autumn in its beauty came and went:
Another letter o'er the sea is sent;
Now Philip writes, " My ship I cannot leave,
Though for each day's delay I deeply grieve.

Dear Margret, when the August moon is round,
I trust at your dear side I shall be found ;
Then I hope, darling, I shall read more love
In your blue eyes than your kind letters prove.

They touch like hands of ice my heart of flame,
But yet I may be wrong great love to claim :
Women perhaps do never feel as we ;
They do not love with our intensity.

How feeble, Margret, is thy love to mine !
Its color is as water to the wine :
Try to love Philip yet a little more ;
My heart and life break only on thy shore.

Thou canst lead up to Heaven, or down to Hell,
The soul that loves thee, Margret, but too well ;
My nature, in its depth unknown before,
But thou hast stirred me to my inmost core.

Thou art aware how dark and strange and sad
My nature is ; but thou canst make it glad :
The needle of my soul points but to thee ;
If thou shouldst fail me, I a wreck should be.

Perhaps 'tis selfish, Margret, so to speak.
Is it my love for thee that makes me weak?
The thought sometimes will come. I am not dear:
I stagger, sink, beneath that monstrous fear.

Give to my sea of love one drop, I pray;
I give a sun of light. — spare me one ray:
Is not my gift a whole. full heart to thee?
Oh do not. Margret. give a part to me!

Pardon me, dearest : thou dost give. I know,
All that thou hast to give : thy love will grow
When thou art wholly mine : then I shall see
How my devotion begets love in thee."

Margret. crushing that letter in her hands,
Pale as the lifeless stone near which she stands :
" My God. be merciful ; strengthen. I plead :
Thy grace and power I now do greatly need.

Thou loving heart, dear Philip. Philip mine, —
Am I a traitress to that heart of thine?
A traitress. I! not outwardly, but here,
Here in my heart, do I not hold thee dear?

Philip. forgive me : I have struggled. bled,
To turn the shaft from thy beloved head :
Blindness I wish had closed these eyes of mine
Ere they had seen another face than thine.

I have not wronged thee by one word or sign ;
No eye hath seen this treachery of mine ;
He who broke in upon my peaceful rest
Has never guessed the secret of my breast.

I felt 'twas not for me to pass my day
In idle pleasure with the young and gay,
When thou wast fighting for thy country's life,
Bearing thy manly part in her great strife.

Most just and lawful seemed that strife to thee :
That war was right, I doubted ; could not see
That we were ever forced the sword to wield :
I thought by other means we might be healed.

I said, But he's in danger on the sea :
Where is the fitting place for me to be?
How can I please and serve my Philip best?
How prove me worthy of that faithful breast?

In hospitals, to sickness, sorrow, pain,
I'll minister till he come home again :
I little thought those walls could wake for me
Passion from which I thought my heart was free.

But there, 'midst death, disease, and sore distress,
Moved one whose office was to heal and bless :
Alas for me ! that touch wrought only pain,
And wound about my heart a cruel chain.

In war, that standard only would he bear;
The healing mission only would he share:
Resolved his hand never a blow should give,
But rather strive to bid the wounded live.

No one could say his was the coward's plea,
For always foremost in the danger he:
He could not *argue*, but *felt* war was wrong;
At least, he could not in her ranks belong.

Daily we met: slowly, to me unknown,
The links were forged, until the chain had grown
So tight, so heavy, that it crushed my side:
I screamed with pain,— the truth I could not hide.

I did not think such tempest in me lay;
I did not know that any soul could sway
My spirit thus, and hurl me here and there,
Now stilled with joy, now maddened with despair.

I saw he held me with a grasp of steel:
But not to him his power would I reveal;
I trod upon my heart, and made no moan,
As if the flesh and blood were wood and stone.

I resolutely turned my face away;
Upon that battle-field I would not stay:
Dangers there are so great, the brave must fly;
Those are the cowards who remain to die.

I cut with ruthless hand each quivering nerve;
Body and spirit moaned, I did not swerve:
I said, This mighty passion shall not stand;
Of my own soul I will not lose command.

I will be true to Philip if I die;
I will not brand my soul with treachery:
My Philip yet shall reign, and reign alone;
I'll put the rightful king upon the throne.

I did not think the step I took could grieve
The heart of him whom I was bound to leave:
Foolish was I to deem the shaft had come
So straightly, swiftly, and so surely home,

Had he not dipped the point in his own blood,
Had it not tasted first that crimson flood:
Directly from his heart to mine it came:
A loving hand takes an unfailing aim.

Am I not right to cling to Philip still,
To keep my faith to him, come good or ill?
Will not God help me tread temptation down,
And to the rightful head restore the crown?

But am I right? Sometimes I cannot tell:
My soul has often asked if all is well;
Do I give Philip a divided heart?
Do I receive a whole, and give a part?

Sorrow must fall on one : which must it be?
My heart bleeds, Philip, when I think of thee :
Thou wert not made to live and die alone :
Have I not promised to become thine own?

Richard is strong ; a soul like his mounts higher,
If in its youth it is baptized with fire :
If the same waters over Philip roll,
They quench the light now burning in his soul.

Richard will rise again, for he is king :
Another heart to him will comfort bring ;
Some weak, frail child, who needs his stalwart breast,
To lean upon, — a home where she can rest.

The waves of Philip's heart break at my feet :
Those bitter waters I may turn to sweet :
That dark and troubled sea has much to tell :
To that sad story I shall listen well.

When the storm rages, I shall speak of peace,
Of Him who bade the howling winds to cease ;
With help of God, I trust to me 'tis given
To make that sea reflect the light of heaven.

Those feet already seek the narrow way ;
'Tis mine to see they do not from it stray :
Many there are who cannot walk alone ;
They must be led, if they would reach God's throne.

A soul must not be sent to us in vain :
Christ gives a solemn charge, I come again ;
Thy brother's keeper thou perforce must be, —
His blood I surely shall require of thee.

Sometimes the only weapon we can bear
Within our weak and trembling arms is prayer ;
Then with that weapon we must ceaseless fight
Till every foe has vanished from our sight.

If I should find I'm weaker than I thought,
That in a hopeless net my life is caught,
Unto his heart I will my own disclose,
And on his generosity repose.

For without love it must be sin to wed ;
We cannot look for blessing on the head :
If love has flown for ever from the heart,
Then own the truth, not act the liar's part.

Perhaps I took a sinful step at first ;
Perhaps such union would be simply cursed :
I will not take a second step of sin, —
Because I took the first, go deeper in.

I'll prove myself: I trust I shall not need
To torture him ; I think I shall succeed
To bring my heart to his dear feet once more,
To love him even better than before."

Nine months had passed, and they had left their trace
In quietness and strength on Margret's face :
She sat alone, and cried, " Thou restless sea,
Peace comes to all ; why is there none for thee ?

Hast thou such mighty sorrows in thy heart
That thou canst never wholly with them part ?
Hast thou such awful secrets in thy breast
That thou canst never find a perfect rest ?

Must thou remember, when the storm is past,
Another is to come, nor that the last ?
Why not accept the present peace that flows ?
Why vex thy o'er-taxed heart with future woes ?

The Seer of Patmos said there should not be
A place reserved in heaven for thee, O sea !
The words fall sadly always on my ear,
So sweet it is on earth thee to be near.

Is it, that in that region of the blest
There must be nought that knows not how to rest ?
That in the realm where storm and discord cease
There must be nothing that refuseth peace ?

Lost in my Father's arms are all my fears ;
I'll trust His strength through all my coming years. —
Yes, even now : my heart be brave ; 'tis he,
Roger, the soldier ; yes, he comes for me."

" Madam," he said, " King Richard, as we call
Our loved physician, and the friend of all,
Has ta'en the fever ; and will die, I fear,
Unless divine and human aid are near.

Last night I watched with him : dreams haunt his sleep ;
He waked and screamed, Poor·watch, in sooth, ye keep :
I saw her pass just now the outer gate ;
I heard her cry, No hope ; too late, too late !

He seems to search for what he cannot find.
He says, She must be here : you all are blind.
I die, he groans : she will not come to me ;
Her heart is with her sailor on the sea.

Madam, these troubled thoughts, to me it seems,
Come from imperfect sleep, disturbèd dreams :
One night of rest this fever's power would break.
Will you not, lady, for King Richard's sake,

Come back once more, and see what you can do?
No nurse so skilful and so calm as you.
Perhaps your gentle voice might drive away
These fearful thoughts that haunt him night and day.

A song of yours might creep into his brain,
Quiet those pulses throbbing now with pain,
And harmonize once more those shattered strings :
Always to him such power music brings.

A sweeter instrument could not be found :
Till now it never gave discordant sound ;
Your hand might strike that magic, hidden key
Which would restore the whole to harmony."

He paused. She answered, "I will come, if well.
I doubt, I fear : 'tis very hard to tell
What course is best in such a fearful strait."
He pleaded, " Come ; and do not come too late."

" Philip," she cried, " couldst thou thy Margret see,
Thy heart with tender pity filled would be.
Shall I refuse to go, let Richard die, —
To save that noble life refuse to try?

Shall I be false, my Philip, if I go?
Shall I forget thee, if I see this woe?
Will my weak heart be so acutely pained
That strength will vanish which from God I've gained?

Perhaps that spirit I could soothe to peace ;
To that imprisoned mind might bring release :
For I have heard delirium like this
Is caused and cured by what the heart doth miss.

If the poor eyes search on, and search in vain,
The body waneth through the spirit's pain ;
If that should come for which the sick soul yearns,
The fever ebbs, and strength at last returns.

I from the first had surely deemed that he
Knew that my heart and hand were pledged to thee :
I find, until of late, he did not know ;
And 'tis this grief in part that lays him low.

Never was braver soul than his before.
This fever struck him, when his heart was sore :
If in his pride of strength, no eye would see
This grief which now has gained the mastery.

Sickness and sorrow joined, a giant slay ;
Against unequal odds the strong give way.
Richard, I come ; I will not let thee die :
If I have wounded, now to heal will try.

For I have proved the power of prayer too well,
That I should fear to pass the gates of Hell ;
I, who thought life a quiet, summer sea,
Knew not the heights and depths that were in me.

Felt my soul mount and thrill and burn and glow.
Thank God, I did not cross that gulf of woe :
I felt the fire singe my feet and hair ;
I started back with pain I could not bear.

The thought of Philip filled me with remorse ;
That sweet affection rushed with all its force
Back on my soul : I struggled to God's feet ;
Under Thy wings, I cried, will I retreat,

Till I have gained such grace and power from Thee :
I cannot fail to win the victory.
Never did soul cry thus, and cry in vain :
I dwelt with God ; peace came at last again.

If man with faith and fervor will but seek
His God, the only refuge of the weak,
The chains of sin will break, and he will rise,
Shaking the dust of earth from heaven-lit eyes.

We can compel our hearts, e'en as a vine,
To bend and turn, and as we we choose to twine ;
And to the tree round which we're bound to cling,
A truer, deeper love each day to bring.

I bless my God that now there is no need
That Philip's loving heart through me should bleed :
For in my soul he reigns, and reigns alone ;
And he is mine, as I am all his own.

And if it is not fevered passion's glow,
But pure affection, it is better so :
My love for Richard would have grown to be
A soul-ensnaring, mad idolatry.

Now I will go to him ; strong through the God,
Who this tempestuous sea with me has trod :
There would be danger if He were not near ;
My hand in His, I nothing have to fear."

Father, the hour draws near!
I hear the battle-cry, and I must go:
I must not turn my back upon this foe;
    With thee I need not fear.

Uphold, and I shall win;
I must not faint nor falter on the field:
Do thou supply the strength my sword to wield,
    And to my heart come in.

Oh! do not let me fall:
Remember all my prayers and all my tears,
Increase my faith, and banish all my fears;
    For unto Thee I call.

I should not dare to take
One forward step, nor dare to deal one blow,
Did I not feel Thee near, did I not know
    Thy breast my shield will make.

Beneath me is Thine arm,
My hand in Thine. Now I can safely look
On that which once my inmost being shook;
    Now I can feel no harm.

My pulse is quiet now:
Its throbbing anguish Thou in mercy stilled,
My breaking heart Thou with Thy peace hast filled,
    Thy seal is on my brow.

Affection's gentle wave,
Which from my heart was ebbing fast away,
Flowed back at thy dread word, resumed its sway,
    Laid Passion in its grave.

    And now I do beseech
That Thou wilt grant his precious life to me;
Body and mind restored, oh let me see:
    Now in thy wisdom teach

    The words that I shall say;
Go with me to his side, and give me power
To soothe and bless him in this fearful hour;
    Now hear me when I pray.

    Our souls in life have met,
Our paths have crossed; now here they must divide:
Go with us both, with him, with me abide;
    Our eyes with tears are wet.

    The shock was strong and great;
It drew the blood alike from him and me:
My wound is healed, I pray that his may be;
    Father, for this I wait.

    No chance it was, I know;
No evil angel brought us face to face:
Thy mercy and thy wisdom here I trace;
    Thou didst appoint this woe,

Because Thou knewest well
A shadow dark must pass across each soul,
Ere it would bow and yield to Thy control,
And at thy feet would dwell.

Let not the angel go
Till on each head, from his retreating wings,
A blessing drops, until in heaven he sings,
" 'Tis well with them, I know."

Margret had knelt in prayer at close of day:
Within a hospital not far there lay
A dying man, it seemed; they murmured low,
" King Richard dies, and leaves us in our woe."

They crept from beds of pain to see their King
Crippled and helpless: all had tears to bring;
One cried, " Will God strike down a noble tree,
And leave a useless trunk on earth like me?

Thou valiant soul, oh could I die for thee!
Thou gentle, royal Richard, can it be
That we shall never hear thy voice again,
After the din of battle, soothe in pain?

And can death settle on that stalwart frame?
What right hast thou such strength and youth to claim?
Touch not our Richard, strike thy dart elsewhere;
I, who have never prayed, bow down in prayer.

Stretch out thy hand, O God! and bid him rise,
The brightest sun that dawns on these old eyes:
Father, he told me once thy name was love;
Now raise him up, — by this thy mercy prove.

Who for the sinful, wretched soldier old,
But this brave boy had dared to be so bold?
In battle once, through shot and shell and smoke,
Through hostile foemen for my sake he broke;

Dragged me from heaps of dying and the dead,
Laid on that stainless breast this guilty head,
And bore me off, watched with me night and day;
Live for my sake, dear Richard, live, I pray."

Two hearts on earth were breathing the same prayer,
That rough old soldier and that lady fair:
Did Christ not say, " If two on earth agree,
They surely have what they have asked of me."

The sick man moved and turned upon his bed;
He looked like one who listened, raised his head.
" The battle turns: the day is ours! they flee!
Wave high the flag! shout, boys, the victory!"

Then he sank back; the old, sad look returned;
Those blue and lustrous eyes with fever burned:
" They win," he cried; " but victory to me
Is from this cruel bondage to be free."

He closed his eyes.   How was it, then, that he
A lady enter at that door should see?
" What sudden light," he cried, " has filled my room?
She comes, alike my blessing and my doom."

" Richard, be calm," she said, and took his hand ;
He yielded like a child at her command :
" I thought these eyes would never see you more.
Was this well, Margret, not to come before?"

" I did not know until to-day," she said,
" That any grief had bowed King Richard's head ;
I did not know that any mortal woe
Had caused these eyes of his with tears to flow."

" They did not tell?   You guessed the cause of grief ;
'Tis well the cause of woe should bring relief :
'Tis often thus ; and even now I feel
A sense of healing o'er my spirit steal.

Your voice has numbed this agony of pain ;
I feel as if your hand were on my brain,
As if your soul were passing into mine ;
My pulses answer yours, they beat your time.

I feel this fever ebbing fast away ! "
He cried, " O Margret ! have you dared to pray
That I should live, I who have longed to die,
I who thanked God to feel that death was nigh?"

She moaned, God help you, Richard, and forgive :
When you are better, you will wish to live ;
That was the sick man spoke, not Richard strong.
Dear friend, have you forgot a little song

I sang to please that English boy who died,
He in his country's ballads had such pride?
You liked it well : you said the thoughts were true ;
You said 'twas more than music in your view.

Perhaps t'would soothe you now, and bring you sleep :
Music gives slumber sometimes soft and deep."
" Yes, Margret, sing the song ; I like it well :
Perhaps 'twill do me good ; I cannot tell."

King Robert lay in the forest dell,
   Sore wounded and distressed ;
A random arrow had pierced too well
   King Robert's royal breast.

Another had borne the prize away
   Which he had hoped to wear ;
And the kingly heart had given way
   With grief too great to bear.

His faithful Herbert essayed to move
   The arrow from his heart ;
But with all his strength King Robert strove,
   And would not with it part.

Thou cruel Herbert, forbear, forbear;
   Wilt thou not let me die?
This wretched life, pray why wouldst thou spare?
   What joy on earth have I?

I am defeated, boy, and undone;
   My heart is cleft in twain;
For my eyes and arms there is but one,
   For her my love is vain.

Let me die, and then I shall not see
   A sight I could not bear:
Their blessedness would but madden me,
   And drive me to despair.

Death comes at her hands, therefore 'tis dear:
   Stanch not the blood, I pray;
For every drop she will give a tear,—
   Let Robert have his way.

She will bend in grief above my grave;
   My death will pierce her heart:
She's cold while I live; therefore I crave
   That life and I may part.

For pity from her will grow to be
   As love when Robert's dead;
One tear from her eyes outweighs with me
   This crown upon my head.

King Robert ceased; but the boy's blue eyes
  With gathering tears were dim;
He looked at his master in surprise,
  And thus he spoke to him : —

I am but a page, and thou art King,
  And yet I must be heard;
The suit is another's that I bring,
  I speak another's word.

That other is bending over thee,
  But thou dost heed him not:
He never ceased to remember thee,
  But thou hast him forgot.

He walked with thee on each battle-field,
  He scattered all thy foes;
His faithful breast was thine only shield,
  He warded off their blows.

He gave thee wisdom and strength and skill,
  He gave thee power to sway
The hearts of men at thy royal will,
  To love thee and obey.

But now He is asking thee to take
  A sorrow He doth give;
Is pleading that thou, for his dear sake,
  Be willing still to live.

He is asking thee to touch the cross,
   Which He was made to bear ;
Is asking submission to thy loss,
   And not this black despair.

From thy life's full wreath He asketh thee
   One flower to resign ;
In thy garland 'twas not meant to be,
   Nor in thy chaplet twine.

The Master planted that lovely flower,
   Watched over it with care ;
He nursed it alike with sun and shower,
   It grew surpassing fair.

He wished to give it to one whose life
   No other blessing had ;
To one whose mind and soul were at strife,
   Whose heart was sore and sad.

The Master saw it was thus alone
   That sad dark soul would draw
Virtue and strength : such power, all must own,
   In love's constraining law.

But, Robert, he made thee strong to live
   By help from him alone ;
Unnumbered blessings to thee did give,
   And raised thee to a throne.

Now listen: his children everywhere
   Are calling thee for aid;
They perish with sorrow, sin, and care,
   These souls that He has made.

Thou hast fought for him in Palestine,
   Fight now for him at home,
That through this darkness his light may shine,
   Here too his kingdom come.

He points to the weak and the oppressed,
   The sinful and the blind;
Man leaves, wherever his feet have pressed,
   A trail of blood behind.

He works in his vineyard all the day,
   He asketh help of thee;
To that loving, pleading voice, I pray,
   What may thine answer be?

She ceased: deep silence reigned, no sound was heard;
She bent her head to catch an answering word;
Only a soft, low breathing reached her ear, —
" Thank God!" she murmured, " now I have no fear."

She watched him long: how beautiful he seemed!
Anon he smiled, as if of peace he dreamed;
She closed her eyes, as if she could not brook
Too long on him, once so beloved, to look.

They all had gone, and left her there with him :
The clock ticked loud, the lamp burned low and dim ;
God and the holy stars were looking down,
Angels were weaving their immortal crown.

A fiercer battle never had been waged
Than that in which those two had been engaged :
The contest over, they who fought were there, —
One in the land of dreams, and one in prayer.

The night wore on, and still King Richard slept,
And still a sleepless watch that lady kept ;
The waning stars at last foretold the morn,
The kindling east proclaimed that day was born.

Then suddenly the sick man raised his head :
" You wait my answer, Herbert," then he said.
" I had forgot : 'tween heaven and earth I've been ;
I've heard the Master, and his face I've seen.

'Tis as you said, dear Herbert : 'tis his will
That I should here remain, his work fulfil :
You said He healeth all who will be healed ;
I bow my head, and to his wisdom yield.

If He has work on earth for me to do,
I will arise, and to that work be true.
Now, Herbert, take the arrow from my breast :
For me, for all, He knoweth what is best."

Margret to heaven raised her grateful eyes:
" Thou art all-loving as Thou art all-wise ;
The darkest spirit can Thy power quell :
God bless thee, Richard ; now farewell, farewell."

———————

Three months had passed : the summer sun rode high ;
No cloud to break the azure of that sky :
Margret had wandered down upon the shore ;
Each day she loved the ocean more and more.

Long while alone she sat ; no sound was heard
But the soft plash of waves or song of bird :
The noon had passed ; the sun was sinking low,
Bathing the sky and sea in amber glow.

A distant step was heard ; she turned her head :
" Old John, the sailor !" then aloud she said.
" Ah, yes ! I think he comes in search of me :
He loves to sit and talk about the sea."

" Good morning, lady." " Afternoon, I think :
Look in the west ; the sun begins to sink."
" Ah, yes," he sighed : " I only meant to pray,
Whate'er the hour, to you might be good day."

He paused. She said, " Why, John, you're silent grown :
This solemn, troubled look is not your own :
I thought you would have much to say to me ;
I have not seen you since that fight at sea.

I know this contest lawful in your sight;
I cannot clearly see that war is right:
I cannot justify it to my mind,
Unless another code than Christ's I find.

But 'twas a glorious victory we gained;
And, though so many hearts are sorely pained,
God in His mercy kept our darlings well, —
Not one of all we loved on that day fell."

" Was it a victory?" old John replied.
" Ah yes, perhaps it was;" and then he sighed,
" In so much joy, we do not all take heed
How sorely, bitterly, some hearts must bleed."

" True, John; God help us never to forget
How many eyes with tears to-day are wet:
But Philip's safe, and coming home to me;
For that I must rejoice and thankful be.

You will be glad to see him here again:
Your wound is cured, John, now; you feel no pain?
You look at me with such a grieved surprise;
And now the tears are dropping from your eyes.

Tell me, is not my Philip safe and well?
If so, what sorrow, then, have you to tell?
Have you a grief, John, and I know it not?
Our league of friendship, then, you have forgot."

" No, lady, no ; ah yes, 'twas as you say,
A crowning victory, a glorious day :
But Philip, he is coming, he is here :
I think, I know, he even now is near."

" Philip is here, and does not come to me !
Old John, what do you mean? that cannot be."
" Be calm, be patient, lady ; do not fear :
I will go bring him ; I will lead him here."

" You bring him ! lead him ! Is he wounded, sick?
Speak, I implore you, tell me, tell me, quick."
" Lady, I will ; then call it, if you may,
A crowning victory, a glorious day.

But, oh ! forgive me if it seems to me
So dark a day, — a darker could not be :
One shot, one shell, that day, too, too unkind ;
It crashed, it shivered, — Philip's blind, stone blind."

———————

Two hours later, on that moonlit shore,
Margret is sitting where she sat before :
But now two sightless eyes are raised to hers ;
A pleading voice her inmost being stirs.

I have no words to tell thee how I love :
          They're weak to show
With what a steady, true, and fervent heat
          The fire doth glow.

I lean on thee; cling to thee like a vine
    Around a tree:
I have no eyes, no ears, no voice, no thought,
    For aught but thee.

There could not be a grief I could not bear,
    If at thy side:
If thou wilt love me, I shall murmur not,
    Whate'er betide.

Oh, leave me not! with thee I am not blind;
    Be thou mine eyes:
If thou art near, no need of sun or moon
    Or starry skies.

If thy dear voice interprets all, then I
    Shall think I see:
Better than sight by far to know I am
    Beloved by thee.

To hold that place in thy dear heart, I deem
    So great a gift,
I shall for evermore in praise to Heaven
    My soul uplift.

Didst thou not say that I am dearer now
    Than e'er before?
Then welcome blindness, every grief that makes
    Thee love me more.

If so, upon these eyes, whence light hath flown,
    Oh! let me feel
One long, dear kiss, that of thy love shall be
    The sign and seal.

" Philip, if thy dear eyes could read my face,
Within thy heart for doubt there'd be no place:
I press my lips against their tender blue;
For now I'm wholly thine, faithful and true.

Now thou art loved so fondly and so well,
Some day I shall not hesitate to tell
Of the dark shadow that has crossed my path,
An angel of God's mercy, not His wrath.

For we can speak of dangers that are o'er,
When we have safely reached a quiet shore:
A soldier loves to paint a battle-field;
He loves the sword he fought with, and his shield.

O Philip! love is sweet, and life is dear,
If God remembered be, if Christ be near:
If they are absent, love works only harm,
And life has lost its meaning and its charm.

The brightest day without Him is but night;
The darkest life through Him becometh light:
Philip, of that great love I dare not speak, —
The theme too mighty, and my words too weak.

No grief must be called grief that brings God near;
Woe is not woe if it but makes Him dear:
If sorrow, pain, drive us to His dear feet,
Then welcome sorrow, — pain shall be most sweet.

Philip, like him of old who could not see,
With wonder thou wilt ask, What may this be,
This throng and press of life?   Who draweth nigh?
Jesus of Nazareth, He passeth by.

Then if of Him thy soul shall ask for light,
Thou'lt hear these words, My son, receive thy sight.
Then, Philip, I shall read in thy dear face
That light with thee has only changed its place ;

Leaving thine eyes to centre in thy soul,
Thence flooding to illuminate the whole.
O Philip ! when He giveth light and peace,
From every sorrow we have found release."

PAUL AND BERNARD.

The moon lies on the frozen snow ;
Does an unwonted splendor throw
On all around, above, below.

Earth glitters in a silver sheen :
A fairer winter's night, I ween,
Than this not often has been seen.

A crystal mist seems to enfold
Each dome and roof and steeple old ;
The air is keen and clear and cold.

Pinched poverty's half-naked child
May shiver at its aspect wild,
And sigh for summer, warm and mild.

But light and heat keep cold at bay,
And make December glow like May,
And turn the midnight into day.

Within that crowded, brilliant hall
Can winter enter, grief appall?
Joy seems to move and rule them all.

Did I say all? That was not well.
What power can we have to tell
What passes in the heart's deep cell?

I've seen men smile who were not glad;
I've heard them laugh when very sad:
God knows what bitter grief they had.

Some think it well to cover woe:
I think they suffer more if so;
'Tis hard against the stream to row.

Some never choose to part with grief:
They loved the tree; the withered leaf
They press, hoping to find relief.

Grief is received in many ways:
Some hearts it tunes to utter praise,
To spend in love their earthly days.

Others are crushed beneath its feet:
They have not strength their foe to meet,
And so their ruin is complete.

How will he meet it who stands there,
Amidst that throng of brave and fair?
Will he have strength the shock to bear?

Will grief to him prove foe or friend?
The gathering storm, how will it end?
Will the heart break, or will it bend?

His face plainly reveals the pain
Which floods the heart and stuns the brain :
A captive he who shows his chain.

A strong, calm face ; somewhat too stern :
A bitter lesson he must learn,
A scathing fire there must burn,

Ere strength with gentleness will blend,
Ere justice will in mercy end,
And soft compassion's dews descend.

Just and upright and pure is he
As any child of man can be :
His life might men and angels see.

But to his feet would sinners dare
Creep with their load of heavy care?
Would tender pity meet them there?

I think they'd turn away in fear,
And wonder why they ventured near:
They cannot look for mercy here.

And yet so true and pure and grand
He looks, like one born to command,
And hold men with that steady hand.

'Tis such a wondrous, kingly face:
Such royal virtues there you trace,
You long that a more tender grace

Should humanize, ennoble all;
Such pure, strong outlines seem to call
For a soft mist o'er them to fall.

But now, as on his face you look,
With pity must your heart be shook,
If pity soul like his will brook.

His arms are folded, lips compressed:
He seems to think it wisest, best,
To put his courage to the test,

And not to turn his face away,
Though what he sees should smite and slay.
I think I hear that proud heart say,

" I will not flinch because I bleed ;
I'll bear the burden, if decreed ;
And then upon despair I'll feed.

I scorn to turn to meaner things,
Despise the solace pleasure brings :
I know how soon she finds her wings.

No ; if on him are fixed her eyes,
And if my love she doth despise,
I leave her to her choice so wise.

A poor, weak creature he : e'en now
The flush of wine is on his brow.
How can a soul like Edith's bow

At such a throne as that?   He bends
Too close ; forbear ! that touch transcends
My patience : now their speaking ends.

She takes his arm, and moves away ;
Help me, my God ! I saw her lay
Her hand upon his arm, and say

Two words that fill me with alarm.
They think me cold and proud and calm :
It stabbed, that touch upon his arm."

If Paul had heard what passed between
Those two, her heart had fully seen,
His fears perhaps dispelled had been.

That night, as Bërnard sat so near,
He whispered into Edith's ear
That she had grown to him most dear.

And when he pressed her for reply,
To grant his suit or to deny,
She only answered with a sigh,

" O Bërnard! if my heart I know,
Its blood towards you doth surely flow ;
I think, I think, Bernàrd, 'tis so.

And then, and then, you know too well !
Your kinsman, Paul, you've heard me tell !
You saw to-night what darkness fell

Across his face at sight of you ;
He, without doubt, is strong and true.
O Bërnard! if I only knew

That you these sins of youth would leave,
Which make your friends so deeply grieve,
You would in time the past retrieve.

Bernàrd, each day some warning voice
I hear, bidding me make a choice,
Which shall through life my heart rejoice.

And to your pleading stop my ear,
Never permit you to draw near;
Bernàrd, they fill my soul with fear.

They are unjust to you, I deem;
For you are better than you seem:
Your life has been an ugly dream.

Your sad, neglected youth I know;
The early, bitter draught of woe;
How tainted blood in you doth flow

From parents' veins, clogging your course,
Keeping you down to earth by force,
Filling your soul with dark remorse.

I see a virtue flash to light;
My soul rejoices at the sight:
'Tis followed by as dark a night.

Bernàrd, you cannot fail to see
How sore perplexed my heart must be
When thus you press your suit on me.

My heart and reason are at strife ;
Dare I trust in your hands my life,
And hear from you the name of wife?

Bernard, to you I frankly own
Unto myself my heart's unknown.
Together from our youth we've grown,

You, Paul and I : both love me well ;
I love you both : I cannot tell
Where doth my heart most fondly dwell.

Sometimes Paul seems to me most dear,
And then I shrink away in fear,
And long for Bernard to be near.

My childish, youthful sins I had :
They always made Paul stern and sad ;
You never thought them very bad.

We could not all be saints, you said ;
Forgivingly upon my head
You laid your hand, such comfort spread.

I was not strong in outward frame :
Sorrows I bore which had no name ;
Such griefs an equal pity claim.

Restless, impatient, oft was I ;
Wept bitterly, but knew not why :
You said, 'Twill do her good to cry.

Paul thought me negligent at school :
You said 'twas hard to live by rule ;
'Twas but the wisdom of a fool

To make all walk by the same road ;
Some needed check, and some the goad :
'Twas well He understood us, — God, —

Who made us, and not two the same :
And yet we all his love might claim ;
He calls his children each by name.

Poor little Edith, you would say,
Weep on ; for me, I only pray
That there may never come a day

When so much grief is in your heart
That from your eyes no tear will start,
Diminishing your grief in part.

One day my lips had forged a lie ;
Tortured with grief, remorse was I, —
Afraid to live, afraid to die.

PAUL AND BERNARD.

You were away, but Paul was there:
To speak to him I did not dare;
His scorn I felt I could not bear.

My soul grew sick with pain and fear;
I cried, If Bernard were but here!—
I think my longing brought you near.

I heard your light step in the hall:
I fluttered down, and told you all;
I thought I saw a shadow fall

Across your sunlit, truthful face;
Meanness with you could have no place,
And yet no anger could I trace.

You said, Come, Edith, come with me:
This lie no more a lie shall be;
We'll own the truth, and then we're free.

You took my hand: the pain was gone
Which had my soul with anguish torn:
Grief with another can be borne.

'Twas winter then, and even-tide:
I walked in silence at your side;
By your kind hand my tears were dried.

We reached the village-school at last:
Oh, how my heart beat loud and fast,
When o'er the threshold we had passed!

The mistress came; I heard you say,
One of your lambs has strayed away, —
Has found no peace by night or day.

Be brave, my Edith, speak, 'tis best:
I hid my face upon your breast,
And there and then the whole confessed.

You heard me right the wrong, and tell
The simple truth, how all befell:
You said, Now, Edith, all is well.

That night to sleep I tried in vain:
My heart was filled with nameless pain,
And hot and restless was my brain.

A light was burning in the hall;
It shone upon the garden wall:
Large drops of rain began to fall.

I rose; could bear my pain no more:
I crept below, paused at the door,
For there you stood upon the floor.

You started back at sight of me :
Cried, Little Edith, can this be?
What pale, sad face is this I see?

I could not sleep, I said, I grew
So cold : I saw the light ; I knew,
I thought, I hoped it might be you.

Close to your side you drew my chair,
Silently sat and watched me there.
What troubles little Edith fair,

At last you said : is not all well?
If not, why then to Bernard tell.
With that, down at your feet I fell.

Bernàrd, I cried, tell me if He,
The great, just God, will punish me ;
That He will very angry be

With such a little girl as I,
Because I told that wicked lie?
Not long I paused for this reply.

Angry with little Edith, no !
I cannot think it could be so :
His heart is pained to see your woe.

4

These great, round tears have washed away
That naughty word that you did say:
Be calm now, little one, I pray.

'Tis time these eyes should cease to weep,
And close in very peaceful sleep:
Be sure the angels watch will keep.

I'll talk to you a little while
And sing, that will your thoughts beguile:
For I must see my Edith smile

Before she says, Good-night to me:
And that Bernard's reward shall be.
I shall not go until I see

This little face look bright once more,
Smiling and sunny as before.
There came a light knock at the door.

You opened it: I heard you say,
Without me, you must go away;
For I to-night at home shall stay.

Bernard, I cried, is this for me?
For Edith's sake, I cannot see
You leave your friends: this must not be.

PAUL AND BERNARD.

You said, 'Tis better so to do :
They are a thoughtless, reckless crew ;
I'd rather stay and talk with you.

You said, Go, James, I cannot come :
A little girl wants me at home ;
A laughing jest 'twill prove to some.

Eyes do not always rightly see :
Unto that little girl and me
A blessing it may prove to be.

Long while you talked and read and sang,
Until the bell, with heavy clang,
At last the hour of midnight rang.

My head was resting on your knee :
You started, and that wakened me ;
You cried, Quite fast asleep, I see.

Come, little one, now say, Good-night ;
Sleep safely till the morning light ;
Tell me the fears are banished quite.

All gone, I said, kind Bernard dear :
You've chased away each ugly fear ;
Oh ! why are you not always here?

When you are gone, what shall I do?
I am afraid of all but you.
Tell me, I cried, it is not true

All that he said, your kinsman Paul?
I heard you talking in the hall,
The day you had that cruel fall.

He said that you were worthless, weak :
Disgraceful pleasures you did seek.
Paul has no right such words to speak,

I cried, you are not understood :
Your Edith knows that you are good. .
I saw your cheek crimson with blood.

You cried, No. darling : hung your head ;
Paul is quite right. you sadly said.
How on my heart your kind words tread,

And make me wish my sins a dream.
And that I could be what I seem
To you, dear, loving child, who deem.

Because I'm good and kind to you,
That to myself and God I'm true.
Oh ! if my darling, in your view,

Bernard is good and pure and just,
If little Edith doth me trust,
Why, then, I think that Bernard must

Try to be good, for her dear sake,
Lest he this little heart should break.
Dear child, you said, I'll try to make

Myself anew, and leave behind
These hateful sins, and you shall find
Bernard is good as well as kind.

Soon after that, Bernard, you know.
This heart of mine was filled with woe ;
For you were forced from me to go.

For many years you were away,
And always seemed content to stay :
How my heart ached I did not say.

While I from child to woman grew,
Your cousin Paul, instead of you,
Proved a most constant friend and true.

But oh to every fault how stern !
I loved and trembled each by turn.
How much of Bernard he might learn,

I often thought: though Paul looked sad
When he a letter from you had,
I wondered if you still were bad,

And weak and wilful as of old.
Bernàrd, can Edith be so bold
To ask you, Did that promise hold

Which to that little girl you made,
That night her heart was so afraid?
Bernàrd, that child for you has prayed.

Oh! tell me what these years have been?
What have the angels gladly seen?
And is there nought you'd like to screen?

Those letters that you wrote to Paul
Did not convince my heart at all
That any blame on you should fall.

I knew that you to him would speak
As if you still were worthless, weak,
And rather blame than praise would seek.

And what was wrong you'd not conceal.
The good care little to reveal,
And so content my heart did feel."

" Edith, that promise which I gave
Made for my sins an early grave ;
At least, from ruin it did save.

Others judged justly, but too hard,
And none had faith in poor Bernàrd,
But you, — your heart did me regard

As something great and good and wise :
You looked in unconvinced surprise
To find I was not in their eyes

All that I seemed to a sweet child, —
Brave, generous, and undefiled.
One day, to hear you speak, they smiled :

You said, He's better than you all,
Him, St. Bernàrd, I choose to call ;
But, Paul, I change your name to Saul.

You are ungentle, cruel, hard :
You persecute my dear Bernàrd,
And without mercy him regard.

O Edith ! how your faith in me
Made me ashamed my sins to see !
Resolve from them I would be free.

Edith, a look in your child's face,
When I held you in my embrace
At parting, still has kept its place

In my man's heart, and made me strong
To battle with the sin and wrong;
And though to me do not belong

The spotless robe, undinted shield,
And though I've fallen on the field,
I rose again my sword to wield.

Sometimes the foe I sank beneath:
Perhaps my sword was in its sheath;
As yet I wear no victor's wreath.

But at my post I did not sleep:
I had to fight my place to keep;
And, when I fell, I rose to weep.

I never broke a woman's heart,
Nor acted any devil's part
Upon this old world's busy mart.

Such, dearest Edith, are the years
Which you have filled with holy fears.
Anointed with your loving tears.

But, Edith, since I have been here,
One thought has filled my soul with fear, —
I think I am to her less dear,

Who used to hold me first and best,
The loved and honored, trusted guest,
To whom all secrets were confessed.

That grief, that fear, has touched my soul,
And other sorrows o'er me roll:
A single woe one might control.

But, when their forces they combine,
They shake a firmer soul than mine;
And yet no fault it is of thine.

I will not urge the coward's plea,
And say I fall because of thee:
My sins belong alone to me.

They rule, because I'm poor and weak;
Upon no human head I seek
The blame to lay, nor will I speak

One impious word 'gainst Heaven, and say,
We're as He made us, — worthless clay,
Unequal to the battle-day.

No : man can tread temptation down :
And, if he fail to win his crown,
The fault not God's, but all his own.

At times, with power o'er sin I reigned :
It seems as if the strength I gained
Is gone ; by that my heart is pained.

Edith, it is as thou hast said :
I did believe the demon dead :
But now he lifts again his head.

I thought the battle ended, done ;
I thought the victory was won :
I thought the triumph had begun.

But once, twice, thrice, I know of late.
I've yielded to the sin I hate ;
I groan to see my strength abate.

This dark, red flush upon my brow,
This restless light that flickers now
Within my eye, — whence comes it, how ?

Because I'm weak enough to flood
My veins with that which poisons blood :
One drop for me is fatal food.

I wonder not that thou dost pause
To grant my suit; thou hast great cause,
For in Bernard are many flaws.

I hear these voices say, Beware!
Oh. do not listen to his prayer!
I do not wonder at their care.

I do not dare to urge my plea:
I leave thee, Edith, loved and free;
I only ask thy prayers for me.

Paul is upright and pure and just:
I yield to him, for yield I must,
Content at least that I can trust

The child, the woman that I love,
To one whom every shock doth prove
A rock, nor joy nor woe can move.

I'll check the tear that fills this eye,
When one too good for such as I
Upon a worthier breast shall lie."

He rose. and left her there alone;
And Edith answered with a moan,
" Noble Bernard! and still my own."

The crowd moved by her from the hall:
She seemed unconscious of them all,
But started at the voice of Paul.

" Come, breathe with me a purer air:
This dance of fools I cannot bear ;
See how they chatter, grin, and stare.

They look like children at a play:
I have no patience with such clay ;
It maddens me to see them gay.

Do they not know man's blood is flame?
Do they think passion but a name?
Do they think life or death the same?

Abysses are beneath their feet,
Above, the heavenly voices sweet ;
And man must choose which doom to meet.

Those two, like dolls I think they look :
Their puny loves I cannot brook ;
My soul is with a tempest shook."

" Be patient," Edith urged, " dear Paul :
Our Father's children, one and all,
Without whom doth no sparrow fall.

In his own way He'll touch each soul,
And make it yield to his control;
To every shore his waters roll.

That face is dull and lifeless now;
But when He writes upon that brow,
With a new beauty it will glow.

I think He's patient when He hears
That empty laugh: He sees the tears
Which have to flow in coming years."

She led Paul to an inner room:
Long while she talked to cheer his gloom;
She thought a gentler mood had come.

" Walk with me, Paul, before we go,
Within these walls where flowers grow,
Though all around is frost and snow."

At her request, they two did pass
Within that house of heated glass:
'' These flowers summer's buds surpass.

They seem to flourish in an air
Too heavy, faint for us to bear.
Why, who is that, Paul, lying there?"

"Hush, Edith; well we are alone:
Bernard, his reason overthrown.
Asleep upon that bench of stone."

Paul, with a scorn he could not hide,
Kicked Bernard with his foot aside:
"Poor weakling, fool!" aloud he cried.

Oh, fatal thrust! oh, fatal word!
'Twere well for Paul had she not heard:
Each drop of Edith's blood was stirred.

It seemed by them Paul's doom was sealed;
And now for years he might have kneeled
Ere she unto his suit would yield.

High in her cheek rose the hot blood;
She like some hunted creature stood,
Defending from assault her brood.

"Hard, cruel heart, such words forbear,
And in my presence do not dare
Breathe aught against him sleeping there.

Have you no mercy, heart of steel?
Can you not for his weakness feel?
You crush men with your iron heel.

You know how bravely he has fought;
You know the victory he wrought;
Some sudden grief this fall has brought.

As yours, my soul revolts to see
This sight; but God forbid that he
Should ever meet contempt from me.

I think of her who once was led
Unto Christ's feet. Upon her head
He launched no curse : He only said,

Go. sin no more. If such as He
Would not condemn, oh ! why should we
With scorn and curses be so free?

Struggles like his are not in vain :
I know he will arise again ;
Break every link of this strong chain.

Pity and love in me combine ;
Strong faith and hope around him twine ;
You stabbed us both : Bernard is mine."

———

That night did Edith pass in prayer,
Her pain too great alone to bear :
God loves his children's griefs to share.

And with the light of coming day
Her hope and faith resumed their sway :
Such courage all must have who pray.

She cried, " This day begins with thee ;
And, ere another morn shall be,
These words, Bernard, shall go from me."

She wrote, " Bernard, do not despair :
This new-made breach you can repair
By courage, watchfulness, and prayer.

You trusted that the foe had fled :
He only slept, you thought him dead ;
He came with stealthy, silent tread.

He saw your sword was in its sheath ;
That you would sink his blow beneath :
So plucked a laurel from your wreath.

We must not fold our arms and say,
The fight is done : I've won the day,
And the last foe I've chased away.

For we must struggle to maintain
The ground we've reached through blood
        and pain ;
No sluggard e'er can hope to reign.

Bernàrd, my heart wavers no more :
I now am sure, if ne'er before ;
Its waters break upon your shore.

Yes, Bernard, I am yours alone ;
My heart is yours, no more my own :
This from the first you must have known.

My heart I give you from this day,
My eyes from you shall never stray.
But mark, Bernàrd, my words, I pray.

Here firmly do I take my stand :
My heart I give, but not my hand ;
That gift Bernàrd shall not command,

Till he can say, Edith, I'm free ;
I've killed the sin that conquered me :
Then I your loving wife will be.

But now I think it would be sin
That holy bond to come within,
Until that victory you win.

Bernàrd, I tremble when I think
Into what gulf a soul might sink
That stands upon such awful brink.

5

Deeds have been done as dark as hell
By those who through this weakness fell :
Go, ask the felon in his cell,

Whence came upon his hand that stain ;
Why branded with the mark of Cain,
Burnt in upon the heart and brain.

He will reply, The deed was done
When I and passion stood alone :
Reason had fled her outraged throne.

Bernard, I trust at your dear side
To walk, to look on you with pride ;
But that you must yourself decide.

I walk alone, if not with you ;
If sundered, Edith still is true ;
Though desolate, I shall not rue

My choice : the child loved Bernard well,
The woman more than she can tell ;
God bless, I cannot say farewell."

The night that Edith passed in prayer
Saw Bernard wrestle with despair :
His grief too great, it seemed, to bear.

Say not that Edith's prayers were vain:
The morning brought a clearer brain,
But waked his soul to fiercer pain.

He paced those solemn fields of snow;
Like their imprisoned ice his woe:
It would not melt, no tears would flow.

All day he fought; the night drew near;
A loud, long shriek burst on his ear;
He started with a nameless fear.

He looked toward the eastern height,
Flashed on his eyes an awful sight:
The sky was filled with lurid light.

From every window, roof, there came
Long spiteful tongues of yellow flame:
Rose to his lips one only name.

The air was rent with wailing cries:
His only thought, " He dies, Paul dies,
The man so precious in her eyes."

He cried, " For her his life I'll save,
And every danger for him brave,
Even though I should find a grave."

" Madness to venture there," they cried :
" If it be so," his heart replied,
" 'Twill be for Edith I have died. "

Half dead, quite senseless, Paul he found,
A trusted coil around him wound,
Lowered him gently to the ground.

Alone, blinded by smoke and flame,
He hardly felt the crash that came,
Or life or death looked then the same.

Down, down he fell ; his long, light hair
Fluttered an instant in the air ;
Down, down, " My God ! " his only prayer.

What followed, Bernard never knew ;
The sight that first did meet his view,
A woman's form, his Edith true.

There dropped upon his face a tear :
He started quickly up in fear, —
" Is not Paul safe ? is he not here ?

They bore him off, I thought, from harm."
She answered, " Needless this alarm :
Paul is quite safe ; Bernard, be calm."

Her woman's instinct quickly guessed
The truth; his secret stood confessed:
She strained him closely to her breast.

"Noble Bernàrd, brave heart!" she cried,
"Then, but for you, Paul must have died;
And now the truth from him you hide."

Bernàrd replied, "'Tis better so;
'Twould grieve his very soul to know
He was the cause of this great woe."

Bernàrd looked at his mangled limb:
"Paul must not know this is for him;
It would his joyful future dim."

He cried, "For you I saved his life, —
For you, who are to be his wife."
She sprang as if he plunged a knife

Into her side, and burst away.
"Bernàrd, what is it that you say?
Can you not read my heart, I pray?

Oh! read it in my eyes, and see
That I your wife alone will be:
God saved your life, Bernàrd, for me."

'Tis winter, near the even-tide :
One hour more the sun will ride,
And then from us his face will hide.

Now Edith tries to work in vain ;
Walks to the window once again ;
Her face is pressed against the pane.

She cries, " 'Tis time he should be here :
It is because he is so dear
Delay fills me with anxious fear.

Oh, keep him safe, dear God, for me !
He comes at last : 'tis he, tis he !
He stops to sit beneath a tree."

Who is it pausing there to rest?
One hand upon his side is pressed,
And heaving painfully his breast.

One arm hangs lifeless at his side :
Its usefulness for ever died
Three years ago this even-tide.

The frame is crippled, bowed. and bent ;
It seems as if the sorrow sent
Upon the outward form had lent

Unto the face a perfect calm,
As if he sang a holy psalm,
And waved in gratitude a palm.

And though it wears a saddened mien,
A nobler face was never seen;
You recognize Bernàrd, I ween.

Not long he pauses 'neath the tree:
" I go; my Edith waits for me."
He lifts himself most painfully.

Edith is quickly there to lend
Her arm; and, as they homeward wend,
The winter's day draws near its end.

" Sit here, Bernàrd, the sun sinks low:
How beautiful this yellow glow!
It seems to warm this frozen snow.

How late you are, Bernàrd, to-night!
Tired you seem, your cheek is white;
You work too hard, it is not right.

I've watched the children in the snow;
You closed the school two hours ago;
You wait to study there, I know."

" Not so," he says, " dear heart, to-night :
I longed to reach you ere the light
Had faded from yon western height.

I met, but, by and by, I'll tell :
Edith, you do remember well
What, just three years ago, befell

This very night, to me and Paul.
And now, thank God ; for I can call
Edith my wife, beloved, my all.

For Paul my heart bleeds on like rain :
'Twas he I met to-night again ;
He has a deep, unconquered pain.

The love and joy, not half confessed,
With which I hold you to my breast !
And yet Paul's grief gives me no rest.

I think he turns from you his eyes,
For he is pure and just and wise :
It seems with hunger that he dies.

I trusted God himself would fill
That starving heart, its sorrow still,
And make it love His holy will.

I in my arms such blessings hold,
It seems this earth is paved with gold;
I've not the heart to be so bold

To say, You ought to be content
With what your God to you has sent,
Knowing no more for you was meant.

I wear the prize which he has lost:
My course is smooth, but his is crost;
I live in warmth, but he in frost.

This crippled body that I wear
Would prove a feather's weight to bear,
Compared with that which is his share.

Three years ago this night, dear love,
Your inmost soul I tried to prove:
Oh, how your words my heart did move!

Surrounded by the gay and young,
Gently the words dropped from your tongue,
And yet my soul with grief they wrung.

Close to your lips my ear was bent,
Back to your childhood's years you went,
And then I felt a deep content.

It seemed to me in those days clear,
That poor Bernard was very dear:
But was he still?   I had great fear.

The crowd swept up and down the hall:
I was regardless of them all:
Your eyes were often fixed on Paul.

You said two in your heart did dwell;
That Paul and I were loved so well,
The dearer who, you could not tell.

You since have told me I was blind;
That, had I looked the veil behind,
The truth I had not failed to find.

That I was first, it had been clear:
It was not I had grown less dear,
But that your heart was filled with fear.

That every voice bade you, beware,
And close your ear against my prayer:
To wed Bernard you did not dare.

I felt unworthy; could not pray
For mercy: rose to go away;
My heart to you farewell did say.

I thought that I had lost your love,
Enough unto despair to move ;
But one more woe my strength must prove.

The riches I had thought my own
Had found their wings, and from me flown,
Into another's hands were thrown.

Stunned by the double grief, forgot
That God is strong when we are not,
And makes man equal to his lot.

So followed that disgraceful fall,
Witnessed by you alone and Paul :
The cause you guessed in part, not all.

From Paul himself I've often heard
How your indignant blood was stirred
By his rough kick and rougher word.

I wonder not Paul could not brook
On such a sight unmoved to look :
With gratitude my heart is shook,

That still your faith in me you kept,
That for my fall you only wept,
And that your love had never slept.

But, Edith, to my God and King
How deep the gratitude I bring:
My life not long enough to sing

His praise who kept me through that night,
Then helped me do a deed of light:
The angels joyed to see the sight.

Such mercy all my love doth claim:
I might have wrought a deed of shame,
Brought ruin on an honored name.

The darkest crimes that stain this earth
Have often in that sin had birth.
What is a gentle nature worth,

When man has kindled in his soul
A flame he knows not to control,
Which unto hell's dark mouth may roll?

I do bethink me now of one
Whose course on earth was well begun,
But through this sin he was undone.

When he had yielded to its sway,
Temptation came within his way:
He lifted his mad hand to slay.

They hunted him o'er land and sea:
Poor wretch! more cruelly was he
Hunted by his own agony!

Blood! blood! no leafy tree that stirred
But hissed into his soul that word:
Blood! blood! it grew a sound he heard.

Caught, chained at last, they heard him say,
Glad that the law must have its way:
His life was forfeited to-day.

Edith, such fate might have been mine;
But round the loving arm divine
Your faithful, fervent prayers did twine.

Edith! that night, I've heard you say
You knelt in prayer till break of day:
To God's own ear your voice found way.

Edith, those prayers were heard above:
What followed did their answer prove.
Prayer moves the God of strength and love.

If Paul that lonely height had kept,
The night that brutish sleep I slept,
His early death we must have wept.

In vain for mercy he had cried,
I could not then have reached his side,
An awful death he must have died.

A bridge of mercy came between
Two nights, or Paul had never seen
Another sun gild earth, I ween.

Quietly broke that morning gray,
To light my Edith on her way
Where helpless, crippled Bernard lay.

'Twas on that morning, Edith, there,
You promised you would grant my prayer,
And Paul's proud spirit always spare

The knowledge that his life was bought
At such a fearful price : the thought
To him with madness would be fraught.

A soul less proud than his might bear
Such debt of gratitude to wear :
Upon his head I should not dare

Such weight to lay : a soul must be
Noble, royal in high degree,
To bear such burden patiently."

"Your thought, I understand, Bernàrd,
My promise solemnly regard,
To keep it sometimes find it hard.

Perhaps such knowledge would impart,
Strange gentleness unto his heart:
He scorns men now, and sits apart.

Oh, if he only knew how sweet
'Twould be to sit at Christ's dear feet,
Even though sinners he should meet!

We'll trust that God will draw him there,
And bow for him our knee in prayer,
And leave him in his Father's care."

Five years have passed. The setting sun
Tells that the summer's day is done:
With this a new week was begun.

The old church crowns the hill in pride;
The ivy-covered doors ope wide;
The people press from either side.

The solemn organ peals farewell,
And prays that if those hearts must tell
Of grief, of comfort, too, as well.

Some have been seeking help to bear
Their heavy load of earthly care,
And begged for mercy in their prayer.

Others have owned their anxious fear
That earth had grown to them so dear,
God to their heart was not so near.

All wend their various homeward ways,
They of whom grief had filled the days
Were those whose lips were clothed with praise.

The last upon that sloping green
Comes Paul, whom we before have seen ;
But now he wears a different mien.

The cold, proud face has passed away :
He looks as if his heart might say,
Mercy for me and all, I pray.

He pauses at the hill's descent ;
His eyes upon the ground are bent ;
He murmurs, " No : perhaps he went

The other road ; I heard him say
That he should go at close of day :
For the same life we both do pray.

Ah. here he comes ! the priestly gown
Is doffed ; the king puts off his crown :
Come, Geoffrey mine, and sit you down.

Tell me. you saw him yesternight,
Danger is past with Bernard quite :
I thought I read it by the light

Which shone all day upon your face ;
You fold him in a close embrace,
He holds deservedly such place."

" The tide is turned. Paul, as you say ;
The fever ebbed at break of day :
He seemed content to go or stay."

" Not so with us," Paul makes reply, ·
" We need him, none so much as I :
How I have prayed he might not die !

Gentle Bernard, and true and brave !
How nobly he my life did save, —
Made for himself a living grave !

How willingly for me had died !
How generously then did hide
The truth, that he might save my pride !

6

And when at last the light did break
Upon my eyes, it seemed to make
The deepest sorrow for my sake.

Unjust to him I used to be,
And only faults in him could see:
He bore injustice patiently.

His one great sin was all I saw:
I judged him by that broken law:
Blind to his virtue through one flaw.

His prayer, Be merciful to me!
I thanked my God I was not he;
Than mine, no prouder heart could be.

I scorned Bernard: I even thought
His sins their righteous judgment brought,
And in his own net he was caught. .

I scorned him, yet I sought him too:
I thought him weak, I found him true:
A subtle bond between us grew.

Though I had lost what Bernard won:
Though he successful, I undone;
Though my joy ended, his begun, —

'Twas only at his feet I found
A balm that did not chafe my wound :
His soothing voice the only sound

Which could interpret heaven to me.
Though I was slain, he made me see
That God a God of love could be.

And so I daily sought his side,
And at his feet forgot my pride,
And even tears cared not to hide.

He seemed the weaker of the two,
And yet from him new strength I drew :
What was his power, never knew.

But something reigned within his soul
Which over me held strange control,
And like a healing stream did roll.

I saw that he had conquered well
The sin by which in youth he fell :
How sore the struggle we could tell

By every line upon his face.
That hard-fought battle we could trace :
A king had won and kept his place.

He never thought his lot was hard,
This patient, gentle, brave Bernard,
But me with pity did regard.

O'er grief his sympathy was spread :
This hunger of the heart, he said,
Is grievous when it is not fed.

No word of blame did ever fall,
He listened patiently to all,
Then prayed, God comfort thee, my Paul.

And do not think me hard, dear friend,
Because I say this grief should end
In time : then will the Christ descend,

And with Himself thy heart will fill,
And every wave of sorrow still,
And drown in Him all earthly ill.

And though thine arms should empty be
Of human love, thy soul will see
Sufficient is thy God for thee.

Then he would say, Paul, thou dost know
I judge thee not; my tears do flow :
I think most natural thy woe.

And thus the man I did despise,
Above all others I did prize,
Precious as light unto my eyes.

The blessing came as he had said;
My hungry heart at last was fed,
My poverty to Christ was led.

And in my love for Him have died
My scorn, my hardness, and my pride:
I look upon His piercèd side,

And see the very sins in me
Which nailed Him to that cruel tree:
I was a cold, stern Pharisee.

Last night I prayed as ne'er before
Till break of day in anguish sore;
It seemed I bled at every pore,

Beseeching God would hear my prayer,
And Bernard's life to me would spare;
It seems his death I could not bear.

I think it was not till to-day
That I could bow my head and say,
Thy will be done, not mine, I pray.

Since then I've felt a haunting fear,
And cannot rest in calmness here :
I'll walk with you, his home is near."

We leave these two, and now we look
Upon a sight we hardly brook,
With grief our inmost souls are shook.

A voice which we have heard before
Moans, " Raise me, Edith, yet once more :
The fading light tells day is o'er.

I must die, dearest, with the sun ;
My course, like his, is nearly run ;
My work imperfect, and yet done.

Dearest, my life on earth is sweet,
I will not call it incomplete :
He summons when He thinks it meet.

And do not raise above my head
A broken shaft when I am dead,
But higher let thy thoughts be led.

He finishes in heaven above
The work which He began in love :
His will we should not wish to move.

Edith, I bless thee; in thee see
The gift my Father gave to me:
Dearest, how much I owe to thee!

My life, transfigured by thy love,
My weakness all thy strength did prove,
My faults thy tenderness did move.

Thy soul with anguish now is torn;
I cannot ask thee not to mourn;
But let thy grief be upward borne.

Think we shall meet, dear heart, again:
Our souls have not been joined in vain;
Not broken, only dropped the chain.

And on that fixed, eternal shore,
'Twill closer bind than e'er before:
Dearest, I must, one word, one more.

Perhaps it is a strange request:
Forgive me, but I cannot rest
Until this wish to you expressed.

'Tis of Paul, darling, I would speak:
Something it is for him I seek;
I must not linger, I grow weak.

He has been very kind to me :
And, when Bernard is gone from thee,
A good, true friend, I know, will be.

Remember Paul and all his pain :
Remember how he loved in vain ;
Lift me up, darling, once again,

And let thy woman's heart regard
His grief, his life ; they have been hard :
Weep not too long for thy Bernard.

But, by and by, I pray thee take
Paul to thy heart for Bernard's sake,
And heal the wound thyself didst make.

I know his spirit now doth move
In harmony, God's grace doth prove :
I ask for him a human love.

To God's high will his own doth bow ;
God's peace is written on his brow :
He's ripe for human blessing now.

His tears will flow with thine for me :
No truer mourner wilt thou see
Than Paul for thy Bernard will be.

We three have grown together, dear;
Paul to my heart is very near;
I go before, and leave you here.

Darling, thou knowest that we three
Walked side by side a stormy sea,
Edith in doubt 'tween him and me.

At last, thy hand was laid in mine:
I felt thy love around me twine,
Anointing my poor life with wine.

We left him there those waves to breast;
We sailed away happy and blest;
We left an arrow in his breast.

He did not walk that sea alone,
A mighty arm was round him thrown,
To praise was turned that bitter moan.

He bore him bravely in that strife:
I wish to round, complete his life:
By and by, Edith, be his wife.

Five years ago, I do confess,
This strange request I could not press,
But do not think I love thee less.

Believe me, never to my heart
Wert thou so dear as now thou art,
When I am called from thee to part.

But, as we near the life above,
Our hearts are filled with purer love,
Our thoughts in higher planes do move.

Affection lives, but passion dies ;
These earthly veils fall from our eyes,
Reveal the color of the skies.

A threefold cord is broke to-day :
I am the first to pass away :
Two must a little longer stay.

O God ! forgive, my soul receive,
And bless, oh bless, the two I leave,
And make their stricken hearts believe.

That to my Father's arms I go :
They stay to serve Thee here below :
Both worlds are Thine, O God ! we know.

Darling, farewell ! Death comes apace :
Near, nearer still, one last embrace ;
Let my last sight be thy dear face.

The mist falls now ; I cannot see :
O God ! my Edith's comfort be ;
Be Thou with her, I come to Thee."

In heaven above, the angels said,
" A crown of glory for this head : "
On earth they moaned, " Bernàrd is dead."

KASPAR AND GERTRUDE.

THE soft white snow is falling thick and fast,
  And through the windings of the darkened street
Sweeps on the wintry, howling, angry blast,
  And the dull tramp of weary human feet.

The bustle and the fret and toil of life
  Are over now, and ended for the day,
Which for too many has been fruitless strife :
  And now they sadly wend their homeward way.

They know for them to-morrow's sun will rise
  Only to bid them wake to toil again ;
And to their doubtful hearts and tearful eyes
  Their labor seems at times to be in vain.

To many sons of earth, life grows to be
  Nought but a constant fight for daily bread :
In this wide world 'tis hard for them to see
  A place where they can lay their aching head.

But there is light and hope in Kaspar's face,
  And, as he moves, his step is strong and free ;
That tall and goodly form a fitting place
  For valiant spirit such as his to be.

That face, indeed, no story has to tell
  Of one whose life on earth is smooth and gay ;
She sees, who loves and watches him so well,
  A shadow in the distance, cold and gray,

Come creeping on with step as sure as slow ;
  It fills her faithless, timid soul with fear ;
She feels it will to strength and substance grow,
  Will reach at last and crush her brother dear.

Now, Bertha does not measure well, we think,
  The strength and courage of her Kaspar's soul :
That is a noble ship that will not sink,
  However high the angry waves may roll.

But now a quiet light within his eye
  Tells of a joy, however brief, to come.
Quickly he moves, the narrow street is nigh
  Our Kaspar's humble, honorable home.

And while he mounts the long and winding stair,
  We will, before him and unbidden, go
To look on her who now awaits him there :
  His sister Bertha we would also know.

No trace of Kaspar in that face you see ;
  The frame is somewhat twisted, small, and slight ;
Though blue and full the eye like his may be,
  That eye has lost its tender, human light.

Bertha is pale, her features sharp and thin,
  Each line upon her face is cut in pain :
In her perhaps some dark, ancestral sin
  Revives once more, and lives in her again.

A frail and tortured body seems to cage
  A proud, unreconciled, and bitter soul :
A cruel battle these must always wage,
  Until they yield to God and His control.

But now as Kaspar's light, quick step she hears,
  Relaxed the lines upon her furrowed brow ;
Though heavily have pressed to-day her fears,
  She has forgot, she does not feel them now.

She moves his chair to its accustomed place,
  And strives to make the fire brightly burn,
And lights a smile upon her troubled face
  To speak her love, and welcome his return.

" Kaspar," she says, " now one might almost deem,
  To see you move, to look at you to-night.
This fearful storm without were but a dream,
  So full your face of courage and of light.

You rise above these lesser, outward ills;
    They lose their power with you, they move you not:
A brave and grateful heart your bosom fills,
    Though hard and narrow is your earthly lot."

" Bertha, forbear, I pray; a song of praise,
    As I moved home, was on my lips-to night:
I cried, O God! how merciful Thy ways
    To me! my path, though humble, full of light.

This room, though small, is wide enough for me;
    It has no power to cramp and curb the mind:
And, when the heart and soul of man are free,
    In poverty no evil should he find.

I have a sheltering roof above my head:
    Bertha, remember Him who had it not.
I never asked in vain for daily bread;
    I dare not — cannot murmur at my lot.

There is a poverty so great, I know,
    Souls wither in its grasp, and faint and die:
They reap a cruel justice here below;
    But mercy, let us hope, from God on high.

Such poverty I pity from my heart,
    And long for power to mitigate and heal;
Grieved that my hands can do but feeble part,
    When for their woes my heart doth deeply feel."

"O Kaspar!" Bertha cries, "if power and will
    Were but combined, it would indeed be well;
And, if the rich their duty would fulfil,
    There would not be such miseries to tell.

But what care they, in ermine, silk, and lace,
    That hungry wretches perish with the cold?
I've seen them turn away their haughty face,
    Then for a bauble fling away their gold."

"Bertha, be just: it is not so with all:
    You but describe a part: pass over those
Whose noble hearts respond to every call,
    Whose life it is to mitigate these woes.

Bertha, be just, — just to the rich and great;
    This bitterness against them is not well:
They strive these growing evils to abate,
    How faithfully their God alone can tell.

Not with the humble and the poor alone
    Expect to find nobility on earth;
Be sure God knoweth where to place His own:
    Oft in a palace they have had their birth.

And, Bertha, do not think the great are free
    From care and sorrow: heavy hearts are there:
Many would take my poverty from me,
    And give the burden which they have to bear."

Bertha replies, " Perhaps 'tis as you say ;
    If you are but content, I bow my head :
I could not but speak thus, because to-day
    My thoughts in that way painfully were led."

A dull, dark cloud comes down on Bertha's face,
    And every tinge of color leaves her cheek :
Kaspar's observant eye can quickly trace
    Some trouble, and he presses her to speak.

" She came to-day ; on foot she could not come ;
    She must be borne in state to Kaspar's door :
She thinks it honors Kaspar's humble home
    To set her dainty foot upon the floor."

" Silence !" he cries ; the voice so deep and stern,
    So awful in its depth of pain and love,
That Bertha trembles : she has yet to learn
    The greater power of him she hopes to move.

" Silence, be dumb !   Bertha, I close my ear
    Against such railing, when the theme, her name ;
One word of bitterness I will not hear :
    Right to defend, if not to love, I claim.

I take no cringing posture at her feet,
    But honor and am just where honor's due ;
My heart leaps up in gratitude to greet
    The friendship of a woman noble, true.

7

I take no cringing posture, as I said,
　And yet I recognize a social line
Keeping our lives apart : I bow my head :
　I have no thought, no hope to make her mine

That line dividing us is weak, though strong ;
　It would not bear inspection ; that, I know,
Keeps many oft where they do not belong, —
　Holds others back when they have right to go.

But now, enough of this ; I pray you tell
　What did bring Gertrude to our home to-day.
Her brother has returned : with him 'tis well.
　Why came she, Bertha ?　Tell me now, I pray."

" Kaspar, your eyes would not see what I saw :
　If I should say what I think brought her here,
On my offending head I should but draw
　Your anger and your disbelief, I fear.

She lingered long ; she often spoke of you,
　The kindness and forbearance you had shown ;
How to her brother you had been so true,
　Had sought his welfare rather than your own.

She said how grateful she should ever be ;
　I wondered not at that ; indeed, 'twas well :
But still she did not go, and I could see
　That there was something more she wished to tell.

Perhaps your brother has forgot, she said,
  The choir of St. Mark's this night do meet.
We look upon your brother as our head,
  No voice like his so powerful, so sweet.

Twice he has not been there : will you remind
  Your brother that we meet to-night again?
And give this to him ; tell him that we find
  To work without him it is quite in vain.

I promised to deliver, therefore take
  The note she left."   He reads, and turns away.
" Will you not, Kaspar, for your Bertha's sake,
  Tell me what Gertrude has to you to say?"

" Bertha, I will, because there could not be
  Aught in her words that should not meet your eyes :
If in her true light Gertrude you would see,
  Her friendship, as I do, would highly prize.

She chides me gently, laughingly ; she says
  I am engrossed with figures, books, and dates ;
I've fallen into sad, prosaic ways,
  And seem contented with the things she hates.

She writes, At that most stupid desk all day
  You've sat: oh, come to-night, and sing, my friend.
If life is work, all work, and never play,
  The rhyme says, Jack's a dull boy in the end.

And then a thought of sadness seems to come :
   She writes, Sing Agnus Dei ; let me hear
Your voice breathe whispers of another home :
   My soul is dark at times with grief and fear.

Amidst a careless throng I act a part :
   They murmur, Gertrude's happy. Gertrude's gay ;
They do not see the heavy, haunted heart.
   Sing Miserere, Kaspar, now, I pray."

On Bertha's face the dark and sullen cloud.
   As Kaspar reads. grows darker than before :
" That letter is not well," she says aloud ;
   " Each day my fears are strengthened more and more.

O Kaspar ! do not give the quiet name
   Of friendship to the love that fills your heart :
You should from her an equal measure claim :
   I fear she does not act an honest part.

You say she loves you not : I am not sure ;
   Sometimes I think you do not read her soul.
Perhaps of that sick heart you hold the cure :
   Perhaps 'tis you alone can make it whole.

If it be thus. then I will gladly own
   The woman noble, and my homage bring
To one who places Kaspar on her throne,
   And sees him first of men, and crowns him king.

The inward eye is clear which can discern
    A monarch when he moves without his train.
That it be so, indeed, would I could learn !
    But much, I fear, she tampers with your pain.

Her woman's instinct quickly reads your love,
    Your homage to her jaded heart is sweet ;
She will not let you from her side remove,
    She loves to see you lying at her feet."

" Be silent, Bertha," Kaspar cries once more :
    " You are unjust to her, through love to me ;
I do repeat what I have said before,
    No nobler woman walks this earth than she.

I see her faults, to them I am not blind :
    You know I do not claim perfection there,
But a large heart and royal virtues find,
    A quick, responsive soul, a spirit rare.

Against her nobleness your malice dies,
    Too little and too mean the charge you bring ;
She'd rather lose the light from out her eyes
    Than break the fibre of an insect's wing.

She does not know I suffer ; she is right :
    I do not, for my life is happier far,
That I can drink a little of her light,
    That in her orbit I can be a star.

Our souls have touched on earth, I am content ;
  She honors me and trusts me, that is clear ;
I do not think God in His wisdom meant
  Our love should always have fruition here.

'Tis much to know her, much to be her friend,
  Whom she will seek in every strait of life,
Bertha, I trust our friendship will not end,
  Even though other lips should call her wife.

Yes, I am happy now ; and, if the day
  Must come when I shall swoon in bitter pain,
I hope that through my tears my heart will say,
  This sorrow has not come to me in vain.

For in my secret soul I do believe
  Most often by these wounds our Father brings
Hearts to His feet, that only thus would leave
  This world to seek the shadow of His wings.

But now I go ; good-night : she must not call
  And I not follow, though the path for me
May lead to grief ; if sure no sin befall,
  I'll do her bidding over land and sea.

If I can lend to her a helping hand,
  If I can sing those haunting griefs to sleep,
I at her side for evermore will stand,
  E'en though my eyes most bitter tears must weep.

If I can be the rock on which may break
   The waters of that most unquiet soul,
And thus my agony her peace can make,
   I murmur not if o'er my head they roll.

If I can minister to that dark mind,
   Give light and strength to that perplexèd heart,
If through my bondage she deliverance find,
   I from my prison-house will not depart.

A strange, strange world! sometimes these faltering feet
   Must tread some human life to reach their God:
When they shall meet in heaven, these words how sweet,
   Thou wert the earthly step on which I trod.

And when God needs a child of His to be
   A bridge like that for weaker souls to tread,
He fills him with Himself: he cannot see
   The work he does; by God his strength is fed."

* * *

     Father, be with thy child;
   Do Thou be strong, for I am very weak;
   Put in my mouth the words that I shall speak;
     I am by sin defiled.

     Help me thy lamb to lead,
   Thy weak and trembling lamb, within Thy fold:
   Thine arms alone Thy child can safely hold,
     Thyself her soul doth need.

Her feet are bleeding now ;
She walks Thy beauteous earth, O God! in pain :
For her Thy blessed sun shines but in vain ;
    Clouds rest upon her brow.

Help me to lift on high
Thy lamp of love to light her on the way :
The night yields not so surely to the day
    As grief when Thou art nigh.

Be Thou her sun and shield :
No earthly light, however bright it be.
Can satisfy ; each soul must come to Thee. —
    By Thee its wounds be healed.

Thus, when the orb of day
Revisits earth in majesty to reign,
The moon and holy stars begin to wane :
    They meekly own his sway.

In their appointed hour
How faithfully they shone and gave their light,
When, but for them, it had been rayless night!
    Theirs was a borrowed power.

O Father! grant that we
May, like the holy stars, shine at Thy will,
And here on earth Thy purposes fulfil.
    Drawing our light from Thee.

And should it be Thy will
In thy sweet service we should faint and bleed,
Yea, if our heart's best blood Thou, God, dost need,
    Let us not count it ill.

    O! be all else forgot,
Save, as with Levi's tribe which Thou didst choose,
Thou art our God; though all beside we lose,
    Our portion and our lot.

Three hours passed, the snow had ceased to fall,
    The wind had told its message and was still:
Well would it be if all whom God doth call,
    Like these mute messengers, should do His will.

The moon unwonted radiance did throw;
    It seemed as if she longed for power to say,
Remember ye who suffer here below:
    After the longest night breaks forth the day.

The peace and light in which the earth did lie
    Seemed to have found their way to Gertrude's heart;
They were reflected in her large gray eye,
    And in that holy calm she bore her part.

Within her quiet room she sat alone;
    She murmured, "Is all well when all is ill?
He loves me not." she answered with a moan:
    "Peace, foolish heart, to-night at least be still.

Yes, I am quiet now; the storm is stilled.
  And over me his strength and peace have flowed:
It seems he with his spirit mine has filled, —
  Has lifted from my life its heavy load.

O Kaspar! in thy sunlight darkness dies;
  To hope and faith like thine my doubts must yield;
And, though the tears are falling from my eyes,
  They gently flow, and by them I am healed.

And if, through him whose strength helps me to live,
  I am in fetters lying at his feet,
So dear my conqueror, I do forgive:
  I murmur not at pain, but count it sweet.

A hopeless love is not the greatest grief,
  A wounded heart is not the deepest woe;
Sometimes we find this sorrow a relief,
  The burden light for which the tears can flow.

The mind and soul of man reserve the power
  To probe him to his deepest depths of woe:
Theirs is the sharpest cross. the darkest hour.
  That mortal man can suffer here below.

A sorrow of the heart I've seen men wear,
  And count it joy, plead with it to remain,
Deem it a burden which a child might bear,
  Weighed with the mind's unrest, the soul's fierce pain.

Now for these sorrows of the soul and mind
    Our God hath opened halls of perfect peace,
Where all who enter shall deliverance find;
    Darkness shall vanish, and all discord cease.

To these fair temples entrance I would win,
    But for my spirit Kaspar holds the key;
My hand in his, then I can pass within:
    To him the entrance at all times is free.

The hour must come for me, — I think, for all,
    When to our God we come, and come alone;
But in our weakness human aid we call:
    We want an earthly arm around us thrown.

That arm of flesh my Kaspar is to me,
    The earthly light in this bewildered brain,
His voice the music whence the shadows flee,
    Rocking to sleep all doubt, unrest, and pain.

That spirit dark which touched my mother's life,
    Which shook so rudely that else perfect mind,
Which made her walk on earth a weary strife,
    Deaf to all pleasure, to all beauty blind,

Has laid its hand, though lightly, upon me.
    Thank God, each day the veil grows yet more thin;
My chains are breaking, I am almost free:
    The demons flee the mind when Christ comes in.

How well I do remember the sad day
  When my sweet mother called me to her side !
A few last words she wished to me to say :
  They were the last, for in the morn she died.

' Gertrude, I go and leave you here,' she said :
  ' God pardon that to you I must bequeath
A shadow of the grief that bowed my head :
  If not for that, I should have ceased to grieve.

For I have felt the cloud lift from my mind,
  As God's most Holy Spirit filled my soul :
Be sure that all who seek their Lord will find,
  Whate'er their sickness, they can be made whole.

I wish to tell you of the friend I found,
  Who ministered unto my soul's distress :
In deepest gratitude to her I'm bound.
  Her image to my heart in love I press.

Look at this picture, Gertrude,' then she said :
  ' Than this was ever stronger, gentler face?
It seemed this weary world she did but tread
  To fold all suffering in her embrace.

Look at those tender, loving, human eyes,
  Open and wide to take the whole world in ;
Nought seemed to baffle her or give surprise ;
  She saw and wept, and then forgave all sin.

Those eyes first saw the light beyond the seas,
  The land of Martin Luther gave her birth;
Not born in wealth, to live in careless ease;
  Child of the people, knowing well their worth.

A worthy child of that most noble land;
  She drank the spirit of the nation's best;
Able to follow or to take command,
  Of joy and sorrow both had borne the test.

Gertrude, what brought that woman from her home?
  I do believe she came for my great need:
She said she hardly knew why she did come:
  But all unconsciously our spirits plead.

I must have pulled about her heart-strings so,
  She could not stay; God sent her unto me;
He does not always let His children know
  What He appoints for them to do and be.

Gertrude, look at that face again,' she said;
  'And tell me, if you can, who has the right
To call her mother. Though her soul has fled,
  She left behind a trail of living light.

Look at those eyes: who bears them now on earth?
  What torch was lighted from that steady flame?
Who can look there, and say, I owe thee birth?
  Who has the right to bear that honored name?

Look at those waving lines of yellow hair,
  What other brow ends in such golden mist?
I think an angel's fingers wandered there,
  And each fine thread most lovingly was kissed.

Think of young Kaspar: is not he her child?
  What other face on earth such glory wears?
Valiant as tender, strong as undefiled,
  The child of many hopes and fervent prayers.

Young Kaspar, filling now a humble place,
  Your father's trusted and most faithful clerk,
I sometimes look upon that royal face,
  And deem he is too noble for his work.

And then I do bethink, The soul so great,
  It matters little what the hands may do :
The noblest in the lowest places wait ;
  They would go higher if they were less true.

Gertrude, five months ere you were born, he came ;
  His eyes first drank the light : e'en from his birth
It seemed as if the baby-boy might claim
  The right to welcome you unto the earth.

One day he laid his small hand on your head :
  He smiled as if the baby lips might say,
If this should prove a thorny path to tread,
  I'll be your friend, and help you day by day.

I saw the gesture, and his mother too ;
  I. smiling, said, Perhaps your child will be
Unto my little one, dear friend, what you
  So faithfully have always been to me.'

My mother paused a moment ; then she drew
  Me closer to her side, and said, ' I grieve
For the inheritance I give to you, —
  The shadow my bewildered mind must leave.

The shadow yours, the substance was with me ;
  Therefore less fierce the battle you will wage :
I weep that even that with you must be,
  I did my best to soften and assuage.

There is disorder of the mind so great,
  We cannot look on earth to see it end :
Mine was not that ; all said it would abate ;
  At last I felt God's healing hand descend.

But still some taint must pass into your blood
  Through me, I feared, though mercy rounds God's law :
He opened at your side a healing flood,
  Whence strength for soul and body you could draw.

I begged my friend to take you to her heart,
  Be mother to her boy and you the same ;
Most faithfully she did fulfil her part ;
  She was your mother all but in the name.

Be sure something of her in you remains ;
 It is the best, the purest, the most true :
The sweetest drop that flows in all your veins
 Is that which Kaspar's mother gave to you.'

Those were the last words that my mother spoke ;
 Indeed, it was for her a happy day
When from its walls of flesh the spirit broke,
 To realms of perfect peace at last found way.

O Kaspar, Kaspar! well hast thou fulfilled
 The hope, the prophecy, those two did make !
But much, I fear, 'tis done because they willed,
 Not for myself, 'tis not for Gertrude's sake.

A truer friend thy mother has not been
 Unto my mother than thou art to me ;
But surely blind the eyes that have not seen
 I am much more than friend, Kaspar, to thee.

Bertha thinks I despise thy humble birth :
 She does not know my only cause for pride
Is that we drank from the same fount on earth,
 And in our tender youth grew side by side.

Yes, God be praised ! I'd rather have that tie
 Between us two, would rather be thy friend,
Than be a wife to one, however high,
 Though from a line of kings he should descend."

A year sped silently; we cannot see,
    Perhaps, from day to day, the wondrous change
Which passes o'er a life; though clear may be
    These eyes, they have at best a narrow range.

No day can pass that does not leave its trace
    Upon the soul, known well to God above:
He sees the slow, sure workings of His grace,
    He hears the faintest answer to His love.

Our grosser vision dates by months and years;
    These earthly eyes to daily growth are blind:
The tree o'er which we mourned, watered with tears,
    Is full of vigor, bearing fruit, we find.

Now Kaspar's face, as quickly he did move,
    Told many thoughts, each rising in its turn;
Now doubtful seemed: he cried, "What do they prove,
    These words? Their meaning I have yet to learn.

She writes, Determined now what course to take,
    But wish your sanction. That is strange for her;
She could not formerly decision make
    Without my voice to say she did not err.

When I review the past, I see how strong
    The trembling feet have grown, how clear the mind:
Tormenting doubts and fears no more belong
    To her; that spectral train she leaves behind.

I did not think such peace would fill her soul ;
  I feared the cloud that rested on the brain,
Though yielding much to God's and man's control,
  Would never quite dissolve in healing rain.

But thus it is ; and now she seems to stand
  Upon a rock, the troubled waters past,
How sweet it was to stretch a helping hand,
  Which she, in childlike confidence, held fast !

The discord in the instrument is stilled,
  The jarring string in perfect tune responds ;
With harmony the spirit now is filled,
  By force of melody has burst its bonds.

How sweet it was to feel that hand in mine,
  To hear the cry for help from that loved voice,
To be the tree unto that clinging vine !
  But canst thou not, my heart, in truth rejoice

That she is able, not to stand alone,
  Too true a woman to do that is she,
But that she finds a strength which is her own,
  Draws life from a far higher source than me ?

Why, yes, for her, indeed, I can be glad,
  And thank my God in truth for her release ;
I cannot think, that surely would be sad,
  That now her love and trust in me will cease.

Is Gertrude happy?   She is never gay ;
   She has the look of one who bows her head
Beneath some grief. as if the heart might say,
   'Tis well with me, though hope and joy are fled

I've seen the soft. gray eyes o'erflow with tears :
   Before they fell. a sadder look was there ;
Bertha has filled my heart with many fears.
   Why do I listen?   How can Bertha dare?

She says a strong, deep love now fills her breast,
   A love unrecognized and unreturned.
How I have longed to put that to the test !
   To know the worst, the best, my soul has yearned,

O Gertrude, Gertrude ! sometimes I have thought
   That it was Kaspar, I, thy faithful friend.
Ah, no ! the sober daylight truth has brought,
   And my sweet dream of hope has found its end.

Who speaks that truth? who breaks that dream of joy?
   Is it not Bertha? — is it not her voice?
Why should her bitterness my hopes destroy?
   Be brave, my heart: perhaps thou shalt rejoice.

Now Bertha flouts the thought that I might be
   To Gertrude somewhat dearer than a friend.
She says that Gertrude thinks to wed with me
   Would be to stoop ; she could not thus descend.

She judges meanly of that woman's soul,
　Noble enough a beggar's love to prize:
Love is too great to bear such base control;
　It clears the heart, though it may blind the eyes.

No thought of Bertha's shall intrude between
　My soul and Gertrude's, as we speak to-night;
And, when the heart of each is fully seen,
　Perhaps this darkness may be turned to light.

Oh, how this hope my languid blood has stirred!
　It leaps within my veins: my heart, be still!"
One moment more, and at her side she heard,
　"Gertrude, I come to know and do your will."

"Rather my wish, dear Kaspar, not my will;
　And yet I wrote Determined, — did I not?
I thought I should your heart with wonder fill,
　That you would say I had myself forgot.

But, no: 'tis only I have grown more strong;
　The sun has risen on my long, dark night;
I wish to hear you say I am not wrong, —
　To know you think I have decided right.

Kaspar, the clouds have lifted from my soul;
　I think you read the sunlight on my face;
The mighty, loving Hand which maketh whole
　Upon the outward form we always trace."

" Gertrude. of strength and peace you often speak ;
    I do rejoice, with you, it thus should be.
Why is it, then, the body grows so weak,
    These hollow eyes, this ashen face I see?

Gertrude, your heart is filled with secret pain ;
    Above it you too bravely strive to rise ;
From me to hide it, you but strive in vain ;
    I read it by my own, and in your eyes.

Speak, and let Kaspar share this grief with you ;
    My hand before has had some skill to heal :
Have I not been a faithful friend and true?
    And if I may not cure, at least can feel."

" Kaspar, I do not think I could refuse
    Request of yours with which I could comply :
But now my own discretion I must use ;
    In part I grant your wish, in part deny.

Kaspar, a woman turns her face away,
    And so from you my eyes I must avert,
When she must own the bitter truth, and say,
    'Tis here, here in my inmost heart, I'm hurt.

I give my heart to one who loves me not ;
    It is a bitter grief, but it must be ;
Kaspar. you turn away : have you forgot
    You urged this explanation upon me?

Let not your heart for me too deeply grieve :
  Remember I have strength my pain to bear :
In Him who loves us all I do believe :
  I lean upon His heart. — find comfort there."

" Gertrude, go on : I did but flinch," he said ;
  " 'Tis natural that I should feel your grief :
I hoped to turn the arrow from your head ;
  I trusted I could give to you relief.

O Gertrude ! is he then beloved so well?
  Is this pale face the sign of your heart's woe?
How long has it been thus? I pray you tell :
  Is there no hope you will this love outgrow?"

" Hope ! hope that I shall love him less," she cried :
  " I would not lose my love to cure my pain :
It is my boast, my honor, and my pride,
  That in my heart such royal guest doth reign.

I'd rather take in friendship that dear hand,
  Hear one small word of kindness from that voice,
Than link my name to any in the land :
  He is my heart's unswerving, final choice."

A ray of hope flashed up in Kaspar's face :
  He bent his head, and whispered, " Speak his name :
Perhaps you are beloved, and fail to trace
  The answer such a love as yours must claim."

He held his breath to wait for her reply;
　　She rose, and crossed her hands upon her breast:
" I am too proud," she said; " cannot comply;
　　You must not put our friendship to such test."

" I will not urge it, Gertrude; 'tis as well
　　I should not know; but are you sure that he
Does not return your love? You cannot tell;
　　Under some great delusion you may be."

" O Kaspar! would it might be as you say,
　　My eyes alone perhaps might error make;
But there is one who sees him day by day,
　　That judgment and those words I'm bound to take.

Ah, no! he is too great, too good, for me,
　　Too far above; I've fixed my love too high."
She did not look at Kaspar,—did not see
　　The color leave his cheek, the light his eye.

His hope was dead. her words the seal had set;
　　His soul to God for strength and mercy cried,
" Help me to comfort her, myself forget: "
　　He took her hand, and drew her to his side.

" I see," he said, " 'tis one I do not know;
　　He in another sphere than mine doth move;
He's great and good, you say; 'tis doubtless so:
　　He must be noble who has won your love.

Gertrude, I do remember what you say :
  I know the arm that draws from God its strength,
Though it may fall in weakness for a day,
  Is sure to win the victory at length.

I know the eyes that take from heaven their light
  Will suffer God at last to dry their tears :
No heart can dwell in constant, hopeless night,
  That leans on Him, whate'er its griefs and fears.

No sorrow linked to heaven by a chain,
  One end in God's own hand, the other here,
That is not lightened of one half its pain :
  God draws us thus unto Himself so near.

So, Gertrude, well with you I know 'twill be :
  Well is it now, indeed, with mind and soul :
It is the body breaks : 'tis sad to see :
  Is there nought, Gertrude, that will make you whole?"

" 'Tis of that, Kaspar, that I wish to speak :
  I think a soldier, wounded on the field,
Should take no shame, if he to fly should seek,
  At least until his cruel wound be healed.

Sometimes upon ourselves, I think, we're hard,
  And in the hour of weakness are too stern :
Our Father with more mercy doth regard
  His children while such lessons they must learn.

I think." —she faltered, turned away her eyes, —
  " I think I'm blinded by excess of light ;
Across the seas, beneath less brilliant skies,
  I shall recover strength, perhaps, and sight.

I trust the day will come when I can live
  Near him again, and yet be strong and calm ;
But now so weak, Kaspar, kind friend, forgive :
  He does not bless me now, he does me harm.

Kaspar, last night your mother came to me, —
  Nay, do not start. —came to me in a dream :
She said. ' All is not well with you, I see ;
  Listen, obey, though hard my words may seem.

My child, I wish you to go hence,' she said,
  ' And leave awhile one who is loved so well ;
I lay my hand in blessing on your head ;
  You will come back, the rest I must not tell.

But now across the seas, unto the land
  Which gave me birth, I pray you take your way,
To join yourself unto that holy band
  Of faithful women, working night and day

To learn to minister with all their skill
  To every form of sorrow and of pain,
That not a wound may gape they cannot fill,
  That not one human voice may cry in vain.

Go, learn of them: the holiest, wisest school
    Christ's followers and earth's sufferers can attend,
And, ministering there, make good the rule,
    In healing others' griefs our own do end.'

She stooped, and on my brow her lips did press:
    ' I have not asked you to forget,' she said;
' I never bade you try to love him less,
    But only to God's will to bow your head.

Love's not a plant that we can prune and trim:
    Only make God the first, His will supreme;
But do not let the earthly love grow dim:'
    She vanished; I awoke, 'twas but a dream.

But is it not a dream I must obey?
    Should we not take our messages of peace,
Come how they will, in any form they may?
    A dream might show a captive his release."

" Gertrude, I think it is the school you need:
    'Twill soothe and strengthen and uplift you too;
You will return to carry out in deed
    The work which they have taught you there to do.

The loss to me, how great I need not say:
    But, Gertrude, will your heart not wish to hear
Tidings of him when you are far away,
    That he is well, he to your heart so dear?"

" Let that pass, Kaspar: write that you are strong
  And well and happy, you and Bertha too.
Be sure that Gertrude will not stay too long
  Exiled from Kaspar, friend beloved and true."

" I will write. Gertrude ; if I cannot say
  That I am happy, I will say I'm well ;
That God is here : 'tis hard to call it day
  When Gertrude goes, and I must say farewell."

———

Twelve moons had risen on the castled Rhine,
  Twelve moons had lighted Kaspar's western home :
He cried, " Kind moon, on her, on me to shine,
  Thou wast with her, and now to me art come."

And when from him she did withdraw her light,
  He cried, " Go, shine on her across the sea :
I murmur not that I am left in night ;
  If well with her, it is not dark with me."

The moon looks down on them together now ;
  Gertrude has come in safety home again :
Both grief and joy are written on each brow,
  They kneel together at a couch of pain.

Far whiter and more wasted Bertha's face
  Than when we looked upon her features last :
The hand of death we there can plainly trace,
  The fluttering breath comes painfully and fast.

" Kaspar, draw near : for I have much to say,
  Much to be pardoned, much I must reveal :
I wrote to Gertrude : begged, without delay,
  She would return, that I to her might kneel,

And beg my cruel thoughts she would forgive,
  My gross injustice, sneering disbelief :
I felt it was not long I had to live ;
  I wished to give my pent-up heart relief.

Look down upon me, Gertrude, with those eyes,
  Those mild, forgiving eyes of solemn gray,
Too meek to wear the color of the skies ;
  Bend nearer, Gertrude, I have much to say.

Something I have to whisper in your ear,
  Something to fill those shaded eyes with light,
'Twill be so sweet, I have but little fear
  I shall be loved again, forgiven quite.

What to your heart would be the dearest sound, —
  The melody most precious to your ear?
Would it not be to tell you I had found
  You are beloved by him to you so dear?

There never was a day in all his life
  He did not love you with a perfect love :
He did not ask you to become his wife,
  Because he failed through me your heart to prove.

My bitterness drew down before his eyes
 A veil through which your love he could not see:
I said you were too cold, too proud, too wise,
 To wed with one so humble, poor as he.

Your noble heart he urged me oft to own;
 He tried to make me just, but tried in vain:
I said 'twas pity, sympathy alone,
 With which you looked upon his love and pain.

I did believe that it was even so;
 My bitter spirit closed my inward eye;
My pride so great, your worth I could not know:
 I did not wilfully invent a lie.

It is the spirit we should guard so well,
 To keep the portals of the heart should seek;
For as it is with them, in heaven or hell,
 Our words do show, for out of them we speak.

I could not bear his love for you to own;
 I could not bear to think his noble life
Had at the very feet of one been thrown,
 Who, as I thought, would scorn to be his wife.

So bitter, so unjust each word, each thought,
 He ceased at last to speak of you to me;
I hoped some change within his heart was wrought,
 Exulted in the thought that he was free.

He bore so bravely, gently, all his pain,
  Never to gloom and black despair did yield:
I trusted that he saw 'twas quite in vain,
  I even felt that the old wound was healed,

The drops of blood that fell I did not see:
  I only saw the calmness of his face:
The nights of agony were hid from me:
  The peace that came with morning I could trace.

Oh, careless, blinded eyes, that see but part,
  Then sit in judgment on the soul of man:
Call a man happy with a broken heart,
  Because he makes of worst the best he can!

And so his sweet submission, all the while,
  Caused me to err: I could not understand
That he could suffer still, and yet could smile,
  And over grief maintain such strange command.

And so, when you did ask me of his state,
  I said that he was happy, well, and gay:
My answer you so anxiously did wait,
  It seemed you did not simply ask, but pray.

I hoped I spoke the truth, and yet did feel
  Some penitence, as o'er your troubled face
I saw a deeper shade of sorrow steal,
  And in your voice a sadder tone could trace.

The thought rose up, Perhaps I judged you ill;
  Perhaps the rich were noble as the poor;
My better nature I at once did still;
  My heart had opened, but I closed the door.

Kaspar. your sister you will scarce believe,
  When I reveal what passed between us two:
She said that very soon she meant to leave
  Her home; her purpose was approved by you.

Kaspar, I wish I could forget that hour!
  You well remember at that time her look:
She seemed a timid, drooping, gentle flower,
  That by a tempest had been rudely shook.

I said that I was glad she wished at last
  To share the burden of this bleeding earth:
In sloth, frivolity, her youth had passed;
  She had been dreaming from her very birth.

And yet, I said, The holiest deeds of love
  Are those not done in sight of all the world:
This step does not the purest motive prove:
  My utmost bitterness at her I hurled.

She rose; no anger in her face did burn,
  Only a growing and intense surprise:
At last she spoke, but from me did not turn
  The solemn search of those bewildered eyes.

'And are you Kaspar's sister? Can it be
  The blood that flows in him and you the same?
'Tis some delusion, that I clearly see ;
  You have no right to call you by his name.'

" Gertrude, no anger could have moved me so :
  No other weapon could have sunk so deep :
Your words my wretched heart to me did show :
  My cruelty most truly I did weep.

No other shaft had reached but that you sent :
  It smote and smote, and stung me more and more :
Unto the one weak spot the arrow went,
  The gentler nature never touched before.

Was I so cruel, bitter then, I thought,
  It could be doubted I was Kaspar's kin?
Your words both shame and sorrow in me wrought,
  Showed to my heart its bitterness and sin.

Give me another heart, O God ! I cried ;
  Make me, like Kaspar, loving, just, and mild ;
Expel this bitterness, injustice, pride,
  And make me humble as a little child.

Help me to see the best and not the worst,
  To find some good in every child of Thine ;
Cast out this spirit, evil and accurst ;
  Fill with Thyself this troubled heart of mine.

And so, at last, my Father helping me,
    I looking up to Kaspar's gentle face,
The evil spirits from my heart did flee,
    And holy angels came to take their place.

And, when the inward eye began to clear,
    I first began to read your soul aright:
When all is dark within, it doth appear
    That all around is wrapped in equal night.

How can a blind eye read a human soul?
    I had been blind through bitterness and pride:
The heart of man, that strange and mystic scroll,
    From an unloving gaze itself doth hide.

I saw that I had failed to read each heart,
    To each a wrong interpretation gave ;
I saw that I had thrust your lives apart:
    From further grief my word alone would save.

Kaspar, you said that Gertrude left her home
    Because of one loved far too well for peace :
Did not the thought, my Kaspar, ever come
    That you did hold the prisoner's release?

Gertrude, was it not Kaspar that you loved?
    Was it not Kaspar from whose side you fled?
That I am right is it not clearly proved
    By that flushed cheek, by that averted head?

9

Speak, Gertrude, now his love for you I've told.
  No maidenly reserve your lips must seal :
If it be as I think, you must be bold
  To own in words the love your heart doth feel.

The letter that I wrote a month ago,
  Beseeching you would come without delay,
That I might speak that which you now do know, —
  How did that letter move your heart, I pray ? "

No longer Gertrude turns her head away,
  Her eyes are firmly fixed on Kaspar's face :
Smiling, she says, " My hand in yours I lay :
  Here, Kaspar, at your side I take my place.

It seems I'm summoned to a bar to plead
  Or guilty or not guilty of a sin :
In such a case, the prisoner doth need
  Outward support as well as peace within.

Bertha, in mine I take your brother's hand :
  I hold it fast and to my heart I press ;
Here firmly, proudly do I take my stand,
  That I am guilty of the crime confess.

Most guilty I, proud am I of my sin,
  Prouder to love your brother than a King ;
Proud that I loved, hopeless his love to win :
  Yes, I am guilty of the charge you bring.

I loved him on in hope and then in fear,
　And then I loved him better in despair;
I did not love him less as God drew near;
　I saw him in my Father, loved him there.

And yet I felt that I must leave his side,
　That I must live awhile alone with God;
That, even as it was with Him who died,
　By all the wine-press must alone be trod.

I loved so much, I felt he was a screen
　'Tween me and God, who must be first and best:
No form, however bright, must stand between,
　If earth would be of heaven fully blest.

I loved so much, I found I could not sing
　In harmony the song God loves to hear:
Through all I heard one note discordant ring,
　One chord too loud, the earthly love too dear.

And so I fled; and, living in that school,
　Striving each day with holy deeds to fill,
I proved the truth of that unfailing rule, —
　They learn to love their God who do His will.

Bertha, your letter found me at the side
　Of one who soon would bid farewell to earth:
She murmured, ' Leave me not, with me abide:
　One at my death, but many at my birth.

I've seen all phases of this wondrous life :
    I have known joy and sorrow, hope and fear ;
I have been mother, sister, friend, and wife ;
    They all have gone ; but God, — my God is here.

Mine was a most rebellious heart,' she said ;   .
    ' Earth was so bright I could not look at heaven :
Woe after woe must fall upon the head,
    Ere such a heart as mine to God is given.

'Tis not in vain the cross on you was laid :
    Sorrow in you fully its work has done ;
And, when a heart true to its God is made,
    Grief flies, because the victory is won.'

Within her closing eyes shone wondrous light ;
    She fixed them long and lovingly on me :
She said, 'At death comes often second sight,
    The dying eyes sometimes the future see.

I see a joy come down from God's own hand
    To crown your head, because your heart is His :
He blesseth those who would at His command
    Resign whate'er they have of earthly bliss.'

Then singing Anton Ulrich's glorious hymn,
    That the light breaks when we enough have wept,
The tired, earthly eyes began to dim :
    They closed so gently that I thought she slept.

Bertha, I read your letter there and then;
  Your words and hers chimed on within my soul:
I thought I heard the angels cry, Amen!
  The mind and heart were sick, but He makes whole.

Kaspar, your hands are laid upon my head:
  That was the crown of joy she saw for me,
The woman loved of Kaspar, to him wed,
  More blessed than any child of earth could be.

She said the light would break upon my life, —
  'Tis breaking now: I look upon your face.
O Kaspar! when I call myself your wife,
  For greater joy on earth remains no place.

Now, Bertha, live, oh live to see us blessed;
  You've rolled this burden from your heart away;
The bitterness and sin are all confessed;
  Health will return, for it we all shall pray.

For you have lived nobility to see
  Is with the high and low, the rich and poor:
Man must be great if there God's spirit be;
  He enters the king's gate, the peasant's door.

For you have seen a heart may be as true,
  Though it may beat beneath a jewelled vest,
As if it by a humble roadside grew,
  When Christ has found a home within the breast.

In different stations we must serve our King ;
  On various errands we are called to move ;
And yet one song of praise we all must sing,
  One livery we all must wear, of Love."

THE END.

Cambridge: Printed by John Wilson and Sons.